HEART OF THE DESERT

BY
CAROL MARINELLI

MILLS & BOON

First published in Great Britain 2011
by Mills & Boon, an imprint of Harlequin (UK) Limited,
Eton House, 18-24 Paradise Road, Richmond, Surrey TW9 1SR

© Carol Marinelli 2011

ISBN: 978 0 263 88672 6

Harlequin (UK) policy is to use papers that are natural, renewable and recyclable products and made from wood grown in sustainable forests. The logging and manufacturing process conform to the legal environmental regulations of the country of origin.

Printed and bound in Spain
by Blackprint CPI, Barcelona

HEART OF
THE DESERT

CHAPTER ONE

'LET'S try somewhere else.'

Georgie had known that there was no chance of getting into the exclusive London club.

She hadn't even wanted to try.

If the truth be known, Georgie would far rather be home in bed, but it was Abby's birthday. The rest of their friends had drifted off and Abby didn't want her special day to end just yet. She seemed quite content to stand in the impossible queue, watching the rich and famous stroll in as the doorman kept them behind a thick red rope.

'Let's stay. It's fun just watching,' Abby said as a limousine pulled up and a young socialite stepped out. 'Oh, look at her dress! I'm going to take a photo.'

The paparazzi's cameras lit up the street as the young woman waited and a middle-aged actor joined her, both posing for the cameras. Georgie shivered in her strappy dress and high-heeled sandals, though she chatted away to her friend, determined *not* to be a party pooper, because Abby had been so looking forward to this night.

The doorman walked down the line, as he did

occasionally, and Georgie rather hoped he was going to tell them to all just give up and go home. Yet there was more purpose in his step this time and Georgie suddenly realised he was walking directly towards them.. Her hands moved to smooth her blonde hair in a nervous gesture as he approached, worried they had done something wrong, that perhaps photos weren't allowed.

'Come through, ladies.' He pulled open the rope and both women glanced at each other, unsure what was happening. 'I'm so sorry, we didn't realise you were in the queue.'

As she opened her mouth to speak, to ask just who he thought that they were, Georgie felt the nudge of Abby's fingers in her ribs. 'Just walk.'

The whole queue had turned and was now watching them, trying to guess who they were. A camera flashed and when one did, the rest followed, the photographers assuming that they must be *somebodies* as the heavy glass doors were opened and they entered the exclusive club.

'This is the best birthday ever!' Abby was beside herself with excitement but Georgie loathed the spotlight and the scrutiny it placed on her, though it wasn't only that that had her heart hammering in her chest as they were led through a dark room to a very prominent table. There was a tightening in her throat and a strange sinking feeling in her stomach as she fathomed that this might not be a mistake on the doorman's part.

Mistakes like this just did not happen.

And there was only one person in the world she could

think of who might be at this place. One person she knew who had the power to open impossible doors. The one person she had tried for months not to think of. One man she would do her utmost to avoid.

'Again—our apologies, Miss Anderson.' Her thoughts were confirmed as the waiter used what he thought was her name and a bottle of champagne appeared. Georgie sat down, her cheeks on fire, scared to look up, to look over to the man approaching, because she knew that when she did it would be to him. 'Ibrahim has asked that we take care of you.'

So now there was no avoiding him. She willed a bland reaction, told her heart to slow down, her body to calm—hoped against hope that she could deliver a cool greeting. Georgie lifted her eyes, and even as she managed a small smile, even if she did appear in control, inside every cell jolted, with nerves and unexpected relief.

Relief because, despite denial, despite insisting to herself otherwise, still she wanted him so.

'Georgie.' The sound of his voice after all this time, the hint of an accent despite his well-schooled intonation, made her stomach flip and fold as she stood to greet him—and for a moment she was back there, back in Zaraq, back in his arms. 'It has been a long time.' He was clearly just leaving. On his arm a woman as blonde as herself flashed a possessive warning with her eyes, which Georgie heeded.

'It has been a while.' Her voice was a touch higher

than the one she would have chosen had she had any say in it. 'How are you?'

'Well,' Ibrahim said, and he looked it. Despite all she had read about him, despite the excesses of his lifestyle. He was taller than she remembered, or was he just a touch thinner? His features a little more savage. His raven hair was longer than she remembered, but even at two a.m. it fell in perfect shape. His black eyes roamed in assessment, just as they had that day, and then he waited for her gaze to meet his and somehow he won the unvoiced race because, just as had happened on that first day, she could not stop looking.

His mouth had not changed. Had she had only one feature to identify him by, if the police somehow formed an identity parade of lips, she could, without hesitation, have walked up and chosen her culprit. For, in contrast to his sculpted features, his mouth was soft, with full lips that a long time ago had spread into a slow, lazy smile, revealing perfectly even teeth, but tonight there would be no smile. It was a mouth that evoked a strange response. As Georgie stood there, forced to maintain this awkward conversation as she met his gaze, it was his mouth that held her mind. As he spoke on, it was his mouth she wanted to watch, and after all this time, in a crowded club with a woman on his arm, it was those lips she wanted to kiss.

'How are you?' he asked politely. 'How is your new business? Are you getting a lot of clients?' And it told her he remembered, not just that night but the details she had so readily shared back then. She recalled all the excitement in her voice as she'd told him about her Reiki and healing oils venture, and how interested he had been, and she was glad of the darkness because maybe, just maybe, there were tears in her eyes.

'It's going very well, thank you.' Georgie said.

'And have you seen your niece recently?' How wooden and formal he sounded. How she wanted the real Ibrahim to come back, to take her by the hand and drag her out of there, to take her to his car, to his bed, to an alley, to anywhere where it could be just them. Instead he awaited her answer and Georgie shook her head. 'I haven't been back since…' And she stopped because she had to, because her world was divided into two—before and after.

Since a kiss that had changed her for ever.

Since harsh words had been exchanged.

'I—I haven't b-been back since the wedding.' Georgie stammered.

'I was there last month—Azizah is doing well.'

She knew he had been back, despite swearing she wouldn't try to find out. She delved just a little when she spoke with her sister, searched out his name in ways she wasn't proud of. His words were almost lost in the noise of the club, and the only way to continue the conversation would be to move her head just a fraction closer, but that, for her own reasons, Georgie could not do. As his date gave a pointed yawn and the hand on his arm tightened, Georgie thanked him for his help in getting them into the club and for the champagne, and in return Ibrahim wished her goodnight.

There was a hesitation, just the briefest hesitation, because the polite thing to do would be to kiss her on the cheek, to say farewell in the usual way—but as both heads moved a fraction for the familiar ritual, by mutual consent they halted, because even in this setting, even with the clash of perfumes and colognes in the air, the space between them had warmed with a scent that was a subtle combination of them, a sultry, intoxicating scent that was so potent, so thick, so heavy it should come with a government warning.

Georgie gave a wry smile.

It came with a royal warning!

'Goodnight,' she said, and as he headed out, she watched the people part, watched heads turn to this beautiful man and then back to her, curious eyes watching, because even that short contact with him, in this superficial setting, rendered her *someone*. Especially, when all of a sudden he changed his mind, when he left his date and strode back towards her. It was almost the same as it had once been, this charge, this pull, that propelled him to her, and she wanted to give in and run, to cross the club and just run to him, but instead she stood there, shivering inside as he came back to her, rare tears in her eyes as he bent his head and offered words she'd neither expected nor sought.

'I apologise.'

And she couldn't say anything, because she'd have wept or, worse, she'd have turned to him, to the mouth that she'd craved for so long now.

'Not for all of it, but for some if the things I said.

You're not…' His voice was husky. He did not have to repeat it, the word had been ringing in her ears for months now. 'I apologise.'

'Thank you.' Somehow she found her voice. 'I'm sorry too.'

She was.

Every day.

Every hour.

She was sorry.

And then he turned away and she could not stand to watch him leave a second time so she took her seat instead.

'Who,' Abby demanded as Georgie sat down, 'was that?'

Georgie didn't answer. Instead she took a sip of her champagne, except it didn't quench her thirst, so she took another and then looked over to the man who never usually looked back. But in the early hours of this morning he did—and so potent was his effect, so renewed was her longing that had he even crooked his finger, had he so much as beckoned with his head, she would have gone to him.

It was a relief when the door closed on him but it took a moment for normality to return—to be back in the world without him.

'Georgie?' Abby was growing impatient.

'You know my sister Felicity, who lives in Zaraq?' Georgie watched Abby's mouth gape. 'That's her husband's brother.'

'He's a prince?'

Georgie attempted nonchalant. 'Well, as Karim is, I guess he must be.'

'You never said he was so…' Abby's voice trailed off, but Georgie knew what she meant. Even though Georgie's sister had married into royalty, even though Felicity had gone to Zaraq as a nurse and married a prince, Georgie had played it down to her friends—as if Zaraq was some dot, as if royals were ten a penny there. She had not told them the details of this stunning land, the endless desert she had flown over, the markets and deep traditions in the countryside, contrasting with the glittering, luxurious city, with seven-star resorts and designer boutiques.

And certainly she had not told her friends about him.

'What happened when you were there?'

'What do you mean?'

'You were different when you got back. You hardly ever spoke about it.'

'It was just a wedding.'

'Oh, come on, Georgie—look at him, I've never see a more beautiful man. You didn't even show me the wedding photos…'

'Nothing happened,' Georgie answered, because what had happened between Ibrahim and herself had never been shared, even though she thought about it every day.

'Three times a bridesmaid!' Georgie could still hear her mother making the little joke as they stood waiting for the service to start. 'It's a saying we have. If you're a bridesmaid three times, then you'll never...' Her mother had given up trying to explain then. The Zaraquians were not interested in nervous chatter and they certainly did not make small talk—all they were focussed on was the wedding that was about to take place. Despite all the pomp and glamour, it wasn't even the real wedding—that had taken place a few weeks ago in front of a judge—but now that the king had recovered from a serious operation, and Felicity deemed a suitable bride for Karim, the official celebration was taking place before her pregnancy became too obvious. Still, even if no one was listening, Georgie's cheeks burnt as her mother chatted on, shame whooshing up inside her. She closed her eyes for a dizzy second, because if her mother only knew the truth... There was no reason for her to know, Georgie told herself, calmed herself, reassured herself, and then her mind was thrown into turmoil again because she opened her eyes to a long, appraising stare from an incredibly imposing man. He was dressed like his father and brothers in military uniform, but surely never had a man worn it so well. She swung between relief and regret because had they been in England she'd have got to dance with the best man.

She expected him to flick his eyes away, to be embarrassed at being caught staring, but, no, he continued to look on till it was Georgie who looked away, embarrassed. She'd had no say whatsoever in her bridesmaid outfit and stood, awkward in apricot, her thick blonde hair tightly braided so it hung over her shoulder and her make-up, which had been done for her, far too heavy for such pale skin. It was just so not how you wanted to first be seen by a man so divine. She felt his eyes on her all through the wedding and after, even when he wasn't looking, somehow she was aware of his warm attention.

She'd had no idea what to expect from this wedding and certainly it hadn't been to have fun, but after the speeches, the formalities, the endless photographs she began to glimpse the real people and place that her sister loved. There was a brief lull in proceedings when the king and the brothers disappeared and returned out of uniform: dark men in dark suits. There was the thud of music and stamping and clapping, a sexy parade dancing the bride and groom down palace stairs to a ballroom that was waiting, lit only by candles, and Georgie watched as Karim stood as his bride danced towards him. She saw her sister dancing, usually so rigid and uptight, now sensual and smiling, and it was a woman Georgie hardly recognised.

As the guests circled the couple the atmosphere was infectious but Georgie was nervous to join in. Then there was a warm hand on her back guiding her, and the scent of Ibrahim close up, his low voice in her ear. 'You must join in the zeffa.' She didn't know how to. Didn't know how to dance freely, even on the sidelines, but with him beside her, tentatively she tried.

She could feel the beat in her stomach and it moved through her thighs and to her toes, but more than that she could feel the moment, feel the rush and the energy, taste the love in the air—and it was potent. 'The zeffa usually takes place before the wedding, but we make our traditions to accommodate the needs of our people....' He did not leave her side, even when the music slowed and she found herself dancing with him. 'Today, yesterday, we do all the formalities expected of royals, but now, amongst friends and family, it is for the couple.'

They shared one dance and even if it was for duty, it felt like something else. To be held by someone so strong, so commanding, was confusing, and to be aware of his observation was dizzying by the end of the evening.

'Are you okay?' He must have followed her outside once they had bade farewell to the happy couple and she stood in the hallway, accepting a glass of water from a waitress.

'It was so...' She shook her head to clear it, the music still reaching them in the hall. 'I'm fine. I'm exhausted and not just from the wedding—it's been a busy few days. I never knew there would be so many things to get through before the wedding.' She gave a wry smile. 'I thought Felicity and I would be spending some time together, I was hoping to see the desert...'

'There are too many duties,' Ibrahim said. 'Come on. I'll show you the desert now.' He had nodded to the stairs and Georgie climbed them. They walked along the corridor, past her bedroom till they came to a balcony door, which Ibrahim opened—and there was the desert, spread out before them. 'There,' he drawled. 'Now you've seen it.'

Georgie laughed. She had heard about the rebel prince who loathed the endless desert plains, who would, Karim had said with an edge to his voice, rather sit in crowded bars than find the peace only isolation could bring.

'You prefer cities, then?' She had made light of it, but his dark eyes were black as they roamed the shadows and when he didn't answer, Georgie looked out again. 'It looks like the ocean,' she said, because it did in the moonlight.

'It once was the ocean,' Ibrahim said. 'And it will be again.' He glanced over at her. 'Or so they say.'

'They?'

'The tales we are told.' He gave a shrug. 'I prefer science. The desert is not for me.'

'But it's fascinating.' Georgie said, and they stood silent as she looked out some more. 'Daunting,' she said to the silence, and even if she shouldn't have said any more, after a while Georgie admitted a truth. 'I worry about Felicity.'

'Your sister is happy.'

Georgie said nothing. Felicity certainly seemed happy—she had fallen in love with a dashing surgeon, not knowing at the time he was a prince. They were clearly deeply in love and thrilled there was a baby soon on the way, but Felicity did still miss home and struggled sometimes to adjust to all her new family's ways.

'She wants me to come and live here—to help with the baby and things.'

'She can afford a nanny!' Ibrahim said, and Georgie

gave a tight smile, because she had privately thought the same. Still, in fairness to Felicity it wasn't the only reason that she wanted her sister close. 'She wants to...' Georgie swallowed. Even though conversation came easily there were certain things she did not want to admit—and that her sister wanted to take care of her was one of them.

'She wants to be able to look out for you,' Ibrahim said, because he had heard about the troubled sister. One who had often run away, her teen years spent in and out of rehab for an eating disorder. Georgie was trouble, Karim had sagely warned.

Ibrahim chose to decide things for himself.

And, anyway, he liked trouble.

'Felicity worries about you.'

'Well, she has no need to.' Georgie's cheeks burnt, wondering how much he knew.

'She had reason for a while, though. You were very sick. It's only natural she should be concerned.' He was direct and for a moment she was defensive, embarrassed, but there was no judgement in his voice, which was rare.

'I'm better now.' Georgie said. 'I can't get it through to her that she doesn't have to worry any more. You know, the problem with having once had a problem is everyone holding their breath, waiting for it resurface. Like that soup...' He laughed because he had seen her face when it had been served. 'It was cold.'

'*Jalik*,' Ibrahim said, 'cucumber. It is supposed to be served like that.'

'I'm sure it's lovely if you're used to it. And I tried,' Georgie said. 'I tried but I couldn't manage all of it, but even on her wedding day Felicity was watching every mouthful I took and so was Mum. It doesn't all go back to having an eating disorder—I just don't like cold cucumber soup.'

'Fair enough.' Ibrahim nodded.

'And as much as I can't wait for my sister to have the baby, as much as I'm looking forward to being an aunt, I do not want to be a nanny!' Georgie admitted. 'Which is what they would want me to be if I stayed on,' she added, feeling guilty for voicing her concerns but relieved all the same.

'You would,' he agreed. 'Which is fine if being a nanny is your career of choice. Is it, though?'

'No.'

'Can I ask what is?'

'I've been studying therapeutic massage and aromatherapy. I've got a couple more units to do and then I'm hoping to start my own business.

'As well as more study,' she went on. Told him so easily, told him in far more detail than she had ever told another, about the healing she wanted to do for other women, how massage and oils had helped her when nothing else had. Unlike many people he did not mock her because, even if he did not like its mysterious ways, he was from the desert and he understood something of such remedies.

And he told her things too, things he had never

thought he would tell another, as to the reason he didn't like the desert.

'It took my brother,' Ibrahim said, because when Hassan and Jamal had not produced an heir and a fragile Ahmed had been considered as king, rather than face it, Ahmed had gone deep into the desert and perished.

'Felicity told me.' Georgie swallowed. 'I'm so sorry for your loss.'

Such a loss. He could not begin to explore it and Ibrahim closed his eyes, but the wind blew the sand and the desert was still there and he hated it.

'It took my mother too.'

'Your mother left.'

Ibrahim shook his head. 'By the desert's rules.' He looked out to the land he loathed and he could scarcely believe his own words, the conversation he was having. These should be thoughts only, and he turned to Georgie to correct himself, to retract, to bid farewell, yet blue eyes were waiting and that smiling mouth was serious now and Ibrahim found himself able to go on.

'One day she was here, we were a family; the next she was gone and never allowed to return. Today is her son's wedding and she is in London.'

'That must be awful for her.'

'It pales in comparison to missing Ahmed's funeral, or so she told me when I rang this afternoon.' It had been a hell of a phone call but he had not backed down from it, had sat and listened and listened some more.

'I'm sorry.'

He wanted her to say she understood, so he could mock her.

He wanted her to say she knew how he felt, so he could scathingly refute it.

He did not want a hand that was surprisingly tender to reach out and brush his cheek. But on contact Ibrahim wanted to hold her hand and capture it, to rest his face in it, to accept the simple gesture.

And he could never know, only her therapist could know, how momentous that was, that her hand had, for the first time with a man, been instinctive. She felt the breeze carry the warm heat of the desert and it seemed to circle them and all she wanted to do was stay.

'You should go,' Ibrahim said, because Karim had warned him about this woman, warned him sternly to remember Zaraq's ways while he was here.

And she did that. She turned and left him staring out at the desert, and as she walked she was reeling, her fingers burning from the brief touch, her mind whirring at to the contact she had initiated.

'I thought you said they were stuffy.' Abby interrupted Georgie's memories, ones she had tried to quash. 'He doesn't look anything like I imagined.'

'It's different there,' Georgie said. 'There are different ways, different rules…' She didn't want champagne, she didn't want to dance with the man who was offering, but it was Abby's night and, yes, it was rather more fun being inside than in the queue outside. Not for a second did Georgie let on to her friend that her mind was elsewhere, but even Abby seemed more interested in Ibrahim than in the club itself, because in the early hours of the morning the conversation turned back to him again.

'You're going over there next week,' Abby reminded Georgie, and gave her a little nudge. 'Will he be there?'

Georgie shook her head. 'He goes as little as possible—he went for the wedding and again when Azizah was born, and he's just been recently. He'll be back in a few weeks when the future king is born, that's more than enough for him. I'll be long gone by then so I won't be seeing him for ages.' She took a gulp of champagne. 'Let's dance.'

And they did.

They danced, partied and Georgie was a good friend and stayed till 4 a.m., laughed and had fun.

Even though she'd rather be home.

Even though she'd rather be alone.

To think of his kiss.

To think of him.

It had never dawned on her that he too might be sorry.

CHAPTER TWO

SHE did leave the balcony, as he had told her to.

Georgie had left him staring out at the desert.

And he shouldn't have turned and neither should she.

He shouldn't have turned, for his mind was angry, damaged by the desert, because when he turned, when he saw her looking back over her shoulder, he saw a familiar escape.

And he should not walk to her, but instead go up to his suite, pick up the phone and summon safe pleasure—for there were women chosen to please a prince or king. They, his father had long ago warned, were his only option when here in Zaraq.

And they were beautiful women and had more than sufficed, he reminded himself, except there was grit in his eyes from the desert wind and there was darkness in his soul tonight. He could still feel the cool trace of her fingers on his cheek and he had never cared for rules and he chose not to now.

He walked to her.

She waited.

She had every opportunity to leave and yet she did not. Her room was behind her, but she chose not flee. She faced the terror and the beauty of the man who was striding to her and fought not to run to him. There was no logic. Only madness could explain it, a charge in the air, a line that connected, an inevitability she desired, because as he pulled her into him, as he lowered his head, she was waiting and willing, and wanted that surly, delicious mouth on hers.

And now it was.

A mouth that tasted not of smoke or whisky but the clean taste of man.

Until now she'd never enjoyed kissing just as she'd never really enjoyed sex. But held in the arms and caressed by the lips of a master, Georgie changed her mind. His mouth pressed into hers, his jaw harsh against her skin, but there was moist relief in the centre and his tongue was cool against hers and made her burn. His hands were as skilled as his lips, because her hair was freed from the braid, and she knew only by the weight of it tumbling. He caressed her long blonde hair as if he was confirming it was how he had pictured it. He smelt as he had on the dance floor, as if he had stepped out of the shower and splashed on cologne, and she wanted to kiss him for ever.

Her fingers felt the hair she had admired as his hands now roamed her waist and just when she thought nothing could be better, he pulled her hips into his, so purposefully, so specifically that for a second she thought she would topple, except he was holding her and the wall was behind her and her shoulders met it as he pulled her in.

She felt it then.

As his mouth savaged hers, as his erection pressed in, she felt all the promise in that lithe, toned body, glimpsed the delicious place to which they were leading. Always she had shied from that path, but she felt tonight as if she wanted to run down it. They could have been in Peru or at a bus stop, they could have been anywhere, and it didn't matter because she was absolutely lost in the moment he made.

It was Ibrahim who had control, because he stopped then, pulled that noble head back just a fraction and looked as no man, no person, no soul had ever looked. He looked so deeply into her eyes that she wanted to climb into him, to dive into the beauty they mirrored.

'Come...' He had her hot hand in his and he would take her to his bed, right now. He would lead her, and soon he would have her, but Georgie was greedy, she was hungry and she could not wait, could not climb a single stair if it kept her from the moment that was waiting to be made. She was out of control and for the first time she liked it, because somehow with him it felt safe.

'Here.' Her room was here behind her, her bed was here, and she wanted them both safe and unsafe behind closed doors, but Ibrahim was a prince and his seed so precious, the orders so ingrained, that he hesitated.

'We need...' His own room would be better. There were discreet drawers, regularly replenished for the women sent to entertain the young prince, but in the guest rooms there would be nothing,

And, yes, they did need. Her scrambled brain, her rushing thoughts were grateful for his care yet she raced to a speedier solution and her voice leapt in delight as she recalled.

'I've got some.' She thanked the gods watching over Heathrow Airport who'd taken the two pounds she'd put into a machine and delivered not the mouthwash she had selected but a little parcel she hadn't wanted, but she was very grateful for it now.

And worlds collided for Ibrahim.

That she came prepared was perhaps to be admired. In London he would not give it a thought, but here...

He did not belong here, he reminded himself.

The rules did not apply.

So why the pause?

Why did it matter?

It did not, he told himself as they moved into her suite, and then when he kissed her again, he didn't have to tell himself any more because it simply did not... matter.

It did.

For Georgie something else mattered.

She closed her eyes to his kiss and tried not to think about *it*, tried to forget and just be warmed by his tongue, which was hot now.

Hot and probing and done with her spent mouth. Now that he had kissed her onto the bed, he pulled the straps on her dress and licked down her chest, his hand pushing up the hem of that hateful dress, but not all the way, because her hips rose so high into him he was blocked. It was urgent, urgent and desperate and completely delicious, her body responding as if it had been waiting for ever to join him. She tore at his jacket, his shirt, her mouth in his hair, on his ear, her hands on his back, her stilettos tearing the silk of his trousers as their legs entwined, wishing the heat from their bodies would melt their clothes so they could connect with skin.

It mattered.

She could not ignore it—could not forgo her strange principle. As she knelt on the bed and lifted her hem as Ibrahim lowered his head, not knowing whether or not it would matter to him, Georgie said, 'We can't…'

He liked her game.

'We can.'

He liked her feigned reluctance.

Liked the sudden shyness as his mouth met her stomach.

'I can't.'

'You can,' he breathed as his hands pulled at her panties and brushed off the hands that sought to keep them on.

'Ibrahim, please…' And he realised then that it wasn't a game. Or rather that she'd been playing a very dangerous one, because he could not have been closer, could *not* have been closer. He was still hard and he was back to angry and for a moment there he did not like his own thoughts, but he hauled himself from her, looked down at his torn clothing, could feel the scratches from her nails in his back and shot daggers at her with his eyes.

'I'm sorry...' Georgie gulped, and wondered how could she explain *it* suddenly mattered.

'I'm not like that.'

'You pretending to be demure was lost in the hallway.'

'I haven't—'

'Don't try to tell me you're a virgin.' He gave a nasty smirk. 'A condom-carrying virgin.'

'I'm not.' She wasn't and she certainly wasn't about to explain to him in this mood about the Heathrow gods. 'I didn't mean to lead you on.'

'You meant it,' he said. 'You meant every second of it.' He wasn't hard any more, he was just pure angry. He'd been told she was trouble and he should have listened. 'What are you holding out for, Georgie?' It dawned on him then. 'Jealous of your big sister, are you? Want a rich husband of your own?' He mocked her with a black smile. 'Here's a tip for the future—men like a little or the lot.'

She was angry too. Angry at herself and now at him for not letting her explain. And she was embarrassed, which wasn't a great combination because she bit back with harsh words of her own.

'Oh, so you'd have loved me in the morning?' She answered her own question. 'As if.' He was a bastard, a playboy and she'd been playing with fire from the beginning, she just hadn't known it at the time.

But there was a beat, a tiny beat where their eyes met.

A glimpse of a tomorrow that might have been, which they'd lost now.

That made him even angrier, 'I wouldn't touch you again if you were on your knees, begging. I'll tell you what you are...' Ibrahim said, and he added an insult that needed no translation and it hurtled from his mouth as he walked from her room.

She pulled up her knees as he slammed closed her door and then pulled a shaking hand across her mouth because how could she tell him *what* had suddenly mattered?

Georgie wasn't looking for a husband.

She already had one.

CHAPTER THREE

It DID not abate.

Ibrahim Zaraq rode his horse at breakneck speed along the paths, across the fields and back along the paths, his breath white in the crisp morning air, and, despite the space, despite the miles available to him to exercise his passion, today, this morning, and not for the first time lately, Ibrahim felt confined.

London had been the place that had freed him, the place of escape, and yet as he pulled up his beast, as he patted the lathered neck, Ibrahim, though breathless, wanted to kick him on, wanted to gallop again, to go further, faster, not follow a track and turn around.

There, in the still, crisp morning, in the green belt of a city, the desert called him—just as his father had told him it would.

And though Ibrahim resisted, again he felt it.

This pull, this need for a land that supposedly owned him, and for just a moment he indulged himself.

'You would love it.' He climbed down and spoke in Arabic to his stallion, a beast who kicked and butted the walls of his luxurious stable, who paced the confines of his enclosure and bit any stranger who ignored his stable-door warning and was ignorant enough to approach. 'For there,' he said to the beast, stroking the rippling muscles, hearing the stamp and kick of his hooves, 'you would finally know and relish exhaustion.' Only the desert could sate. Again Ibrahim glimpsed it—the endless dunes, the fresh canvas the shifting desert provided each morning. He did not just glimpse it, he felt the sting of sand on his cheeks, the scarf around his mouth, the power of a horse unleashed between his thighs.

Yet his life was in London.

A life he had created, business and riches that came with no rules attached, because he had built them and they were his. His mother was here—forbidden to return to Zaraq because decades ago she had broken the rules.

'I'll take him, Ibrahim.' A young stablegirl he sometimes bedded made her way over and he handed her the reins. Ibrahim saw the invitation in her eyes, and perhaps that would help, he thought, as she unstrapped the saddle. Ibrahim took the weight of it from her, saw her hands soothe the angry beast, saw the stretch of her thighs as she put on the horse blanket. He waited and wanted to feel something, for it would have been easier, so much easier to soothe the burn of his body and the turmoil in his mind with his favourite solution. 'Is there anything I can do for you?' Hopeful, beautiful, available, she turned to him—and the answer on any other morning would have been yes.

It wasn't today.

Neither had it been the other night.

After seeing Georgie, he had directed his driver to his date's home instead of his and had declined her invitation to come in.

'Come to bed, Ibrahim.' Her mouth and her hands had moved to persuade but Ibrahim had brushed her off and when tears hadn't worked, she'd got angry. 'It's that tart from the nightclub that's changed things, isn't it?'

'No,' Ibrahim had said coolly. 'It's entirely you.'

'Ibrahim?' The stablegirl smiled and he looked down at her breasts, which were pert and pretty. He gauged the length of her hair and then walked away because, though her hair was dark, it was long and thick and her frame too was slender. Ibrahim knew he'd have only been thinking of her.

Of Georgie.

He did not want to think of her and his mind turned to the desert instead.

He picked up pace, his boots ringing across the yard. He would go to his property in the country this weekend, for he knew if he was in London he would end up calling Georgie. He did not like unfinished business, did not like to be told no, and seeing her again had inflamed things, but more trouble with his family was the last thing he needed now. The country was a good option—there he would find space, there he could ride for ever, except as he climbed into his sports car he glanced at the sat-nav and felt as if he were staring at an aerial map. He could see the fields, the houses, the hedges, the trees, the borders...

And his father had been right, and so too his brothers, who had told him that one day the desert would call him.

The king had let his son go with surprising ease when he had left to study engineering, confident that when the time was right he would return.

'Of course I will be back.' Surly, arrogant, back from his compulsory stint in the military, a young Ibrahim had been ready for London. 'I will visit.'

'You will be back as a royal prince to share your new knowledge, and your country will be waiting.'

'No.' Ibrahim had shaken his head. 'For formal functions occasionally I will return and, of course, to see my family…' His father did not seem to understand, so he had spelt it out. 'My life will be in London.'

But the king had just smiled. 'Ibrahim, you are going to study engineering. Remember as a child all the plans you had for this country of ours, all you could do for the people.'

'I was a child.'

'And now you are a man—you get to make real your dreams. When it is time, you will come back to where you belong.' Ibrahim had rolled his eyes but the king had just smiled. 'It is in your blood, in your DNA. You may not want to listen to your father, but the desert has its own call—one you cannot ignore.'

He wanted to ignore it.

For years now he had, but everything had changed when he'd returned for the wedding.

Ibrahim sped the car through the grey Sunday

morning, out of the city and into the country. He hugged tight bends and accelerated out of them. His father's patience was running out, his future awaited him and he raced from it till his tank was almost empty and again rules rushed in.

'Breathe till I tell you to stop,' the policeman ordered, and Ibrahim did. He even emptied out his pockets and let the man inspect his boot. He saw the suspicion in the officer's eyes when everything turned up clean.

'Where are you going in such a hurry?' the officer asked again. He had seen Ibrahim's driver's licence and was sick of the rich and the young royals who thought the laws did not apply to them. This man was both.

'I don't know,' Ibrahim answered again. Normally it would have incensed the policeman, normally he would have headed back to the car to perform another slow check just to make the prince wait because a fine would not trouble him, but there was something in Ibrahim's voice that made the policeman hesitate. There was a hint of confusion in this arrogant, aloof man's tone that halted him. 'I'm sorry.' The officer frowned at Ibrahim's apology. 'I apologise for not following your laws.'

'They're there for your own protection.' And Ibrahim closed his eyes because, albeit in English now, those were the words that had swaddled him through child-hood, through teenage years and into adulthood.

'I appreciate that,' Ibrahim said, then opened his eyes to the concerned face of the policeman. 'Again I apologise.'

'Is everything okay, sir?'

'Everything is fine.'

'I'll let you go with a warning this time.'

He would rather have the ticket.

As he climbed back into the car, Ibrahim would far rather have paid his dues, accepted the punishment, and it had nothing at all to do with the fact he could afford to—he did not want favours.

Ibrahim drove sensibly, even when the police car left him as he turned into the petrol station. Ibrahim stayed within the speed limit all the way back to London, and as he turned into the smart West London street he did not look at the stylish three-storey house but at the railings in front of it, and the neatly trimmed hedge, to the houses either side and the next house and the next, and he couldn't bring himself to go in.

Had the policeman been behind him he would have pulled him over again, for Ibrahim executed a highly illegal U-turn and then reprogrammed his sat-nav. His decision was made.

He would get it out of his system once and for all.

The future king was due to be born in a few weeks' time and he certainly didn't want to get caught up in all that. He would ride his horses in the ocean and desert for a few days, hear what his father had to say and then he would return to London.

To home, Ibrahim corrected himself.

Despite what his father said, London *was* his home.

He just had to be sure of it.

His mind flicked to Georgie, to unfinished business,

to a woman who did not want the desert, who had been on his mind for far too long now, and another decision was made…he would visit the desert and return, and *then* he might call her.

CHAPTER FOUR

THERE was a new lightness to Georgie as she took out her blonde hair from its ponytail and combed it, and there was a smile on her lips as she applied lip balm. Not even the prospect of the long flight ahead could dim a world that suddenly felt just a little more right.

That her divorce had come through that morning might not seem to many something to be pleased about, and a marriage that had been a mistake might seem nothing to be grateful for, but it had taught her a lot.

Even though she had left him years ago—left a marriage of just a few weeks—the fact it was officially over brought her relief.

Now she was free.

Her only regret was that it hadn't come through sooner. That the morals that kept her from sleeping with anyone, even with her divorce pending, had kept her from Ibrahim that night.

Georgie closed her eyes for a moment, told herself not to go there—it was a path she had chosen. Her illness, her father's abuse, a marriage that had seemed an escape—it would be so easy to look back with regret, yet she had learnt so much from it all. She had grown into a strong woman, a confident woman who knew herself, because she had chosen to learn from, rather than rue, her mistakes. It was a hard path to follow but, for Georgie, the right one. Guilt and regret had led her to troubled places, but no more. She wanted to talk with Felicity, wanted to thank her for all her support through the difficult years. Georgie swallowed, because she was still undecided, but she wanted to tell Felicity about Mike, to clear the past and make way for a glorious future.

Ibrahim's apology had helped too.

It had been unsettling seeing him, of course, but she took his apology as a sign that the chapter was closed and that it was time to move on.

To have no regrets.

The air ticket her sister Felicity had sent meant she bypassed the nightmare queues at Heathrow. She sat, awkward at first, in a first-class departure lounge, but as she sipped champagne and checked her emails, it was soon easy to relax. She accepted the delicacies on offer without thought. A new smile spread across her face as she realised just how far she had come. The endless abacus was finally silent—no more calories versus tread-mill, no penance for pleasure, just the sweet taste of a pistachio macaroon dissolving on her tongue. She didn't need a plane to fly to Zaraq. Her mood was so buoyant as she boarded, her high so palpable, Georgie could have flown there on happiness alone. Finally, the dark days were over—the soul-searching, the introspection, the agony of healing was behind her. She was ready to move on, even if the plane wasn't.

Just a little nervous of flying, Georgie took a vial of melissa oil from her bag and massaged a drop into her temples. The attendant offered her another drink, but Georgie didn't want one. 'When are we taking off?' Used to economy class, Georgie half expected to be speaking to thin air by the time the words were out, or at best to receive a brusque answer, but she was reminded she was travelling first class when the attendant smiled and lingered. 'We're sorry for the delay but we have an unexpected passenger. He shouldn't be too much longer…' But even in first class there was a pecking order, because the attendant's voice trailed off and Georgie was no longer the focus of her attention. She watched as the woman's cheeks darkened. Curious, Georgie followed the woman's gaze and her heart seemed to stop as all efforts to move on were halted, any chance of forgetting lost.

'Your Highness.' The attendant curtsied as he strode past but even she couldn't halt the flicker of confusion on her smooth brow at their passenger's attire. He was dressed in mud-splattered white jodhpurs and black jumper, and there was a restlessness to him, a wild energy that seemed to have boarded the plane along with him. He didn't respond to the attendant, neither did he glance in Georgie's direction. There was such purpose to his stride it looked as if he was heading for the cockpit, prepared to fly the plane himself, but at the last minute he turned and, yes, there were levels of first class because it would appear Ibrahim had his own suite. The attendants fluttered away from their charges and gathered together to discuss the latest arrival, and just a moment or so later a steward slipped into the suite with a bottle of brandy as the others watched.

She wanted to stand, to stop the plane that was now taxiing along the runway, to get off, for she could not face being there with him.

She didn't even notice the plane rise off the ground, or dinner being served, her mind consumed by her fellow passenger. 'Is everything okay, Miss Anderson?' The flight attendant removed her plates untouched and Georgie just nodded, too stunned to answer, let alone eat. The thought of being back in the palace with him, of being in such close proximity to him, had her reeling.

She had done everything possible to ensure that he wouldn't be there—oh, so casually asking her sister about his movements—and even in the nightclub he had given no clue.

But, then, neither had she.

Maybe there had been an emergency. His father had recently been sick after all. Why else would he be boarding a plane dressed like that? Or maybe this was how the rich lived, Georgie pondered. Who flew long haul in riding boots? Maybe he was so laid-back about travelling that he didn't even give it a thought. He could step off a horse and onto a plane… But later, when she got up to go to the toilet, a steward was coming out of his suite carrying a laden tray and shaking her head. Georgie got a glimpse of Ibrahim before the doors to

his suite were closed—he lay sprawled out on the bed.
He hadn't bothered with the gold pyjamas Georgie had
on. He was unshaven, boots off, sprawled out on a bed
and fast asleep.

She got only the briefest look as the door was quickly
closed, but it was an image that stayed with her through
the flight.

Anguished.

Even in sleep his face wasn't relaxed. His full mouth
was tense. Even at rest he somehow looked troubled—
but more worrying than that was just how much Georgie
wanted to know what was on his mind

She'd been looking forward to the luxurious bed the
airline offered in first class, had been looking forward
to stretching out and sleeping, but knowing he was so
close she found she couldn't.

'Can I get you anything?' the attendant asked count-
less times through the flight, and each time Georgie bit
her lip on her true answer.

Him, she wanted to respond. Can you take me to
him? But instead she shook her head and tried to work
out what she'd say when she saw him.

The flight was broken by a stop in Abu Dhabi and
Georgie took the chance to stretch her legs. She braced
herself to face him, but Ibrahim must have decided to
stay on the plane so she amused herself watching the
gorgeous attendants boarding with designer bags, one
even carrying a large pink teddy. This time, when the
plane took off, finally Georgie fell asleep, except there

was no respite. Her dreams were flooded with thoughts of him.

'Miss Anderson, would you like some breakfast before we prepare for landing?' The attendant woke her. Georgie nodded, and felt just a slight wobble of guilt: she had always kept her name, though used Ms in London. Felicity had booked her ticket and, given she had no idea about the brief marriage, had naturally put Miss.

Georgie stared out of the window at the glorious blue waters and as the plane banked gently to the right she caught the first glimpses of Zaraq—the endless golden desert giving way to sandy-colored villages and domed buildings. The plane swept along the shoreline, the cabin lights dimming. The palace that would be her home for the next couple of weeks wasn't what grabbed her attention. Instead it was the mirrored skyscrapers of the capital Zaraqua that made her breath tight in her chest. There were pools and bridges seemingly suspended in mid-air and Georgie marvelled at their design rather than think of him. She tried not to guess his reaction when she exited the plane and they finally came face to face.

He didn't get off.

For a little while she wondered if somehow she'd imagined him, for not once during the flight had she seen him.

'Georgie!' Felicity looked great. Georgie had wondered how she'd be dressed, but as a married woman her sister did not need to wear a veil and looked stunning in a white linen trouser suit, her hair longer than Georgie had ever see it. Felicity oozed happiness and good health, but it was little Azizah who enthralled Georgie from the moment she landed—her niece, just a few months old and with the fascinating mix of her mother's blonde hair and her father's black eyes. Azizah had been just a couple of weeks old when Karim and Felicity had brought her to the UK for a brief visit, but she was her own little person now and, for Georgie, the love was instant.

'She's stunning.' Georgie said as she held her in the VIP lounge. 'I can't wait to get to know her. Where's Karim?'

'He's here. We had a call from the airline a couple of hours ago—it would seem his brother was on the same flight as you. He's gone to meet him.'

'I thought I saw him,' Georgie said carefully, 'though he didn't see me. Is everything okay?'

'Of course it is.' Felicity said. 'Why do you ask?'

'No real reason. I just wondered if he'd dashed back for an emergency. He looked…' Her voice trailed off and she chose not to tell her sister after all. Felicity would see for herself soon and could make up her own mind.

'Karim might have to dash off once we get home,' Felicity explained as Georgie fussed over her niece. 'There's a bit of health scare with the Bedouins. You know how much work he does for them.'

Georgie nodded. 'Is he still doing the mobile clinics?'

'Shh,' Felicity warned, because no one, not even the

king, knew the full extent of Karim's involvement with the local people. We'll talk about it later. I just want you to understand if he has to suddenly leave—I don't want you to think he's not thrilled that you're here.' She smiled suddenly. 'Here they are now!'

As Karim and Ibrahim entered the lounge, Georgie was glad she hadn't aired her concerns to her sister. She'd have looked like a liar because Ibrahim looked far from troubled and unkempt now—clean-shaven, dressed in linen trousers and jacket, sleek sunglasses on, he looked every bit a first-class passenger as he walked towards with his brother, carrying the large pink teddy Georgie had seen the attendants bring on the plane. He must have sent them shopping, Georgie realised, watching as his jaw tightened at the sight of her—not that Felicity noticed the tension.

'Thank you, Ibrahim.' Felicity took the huge teddy. 'Did you have to book another seat for her?'

'Georgie!' Karim kissed the cheek of his sister-in-law. 'You may remember Ibrahim from the wedding.'

'Of course.' Georgie gave a smile but he didn't immediately return it. All she could see was her reflection in his glasses. She couldn't read his eyes.

'I wasn't aware you were visiting.' Only then did he manage to force a smile. 'It is nice of you all to come and greet me,' Ibrahim said, 'but it was completely unnecessary. I didn't want a fuss, it's just a brief visit.'

'We're not here to fuss over you!' Felicity grinned. 'We're actually here to greet Georgie—she was on your flight.'

And Georgie was positive, completely positive that his dark skin paled, that behind those thick sunglasses, even if she couldn't see it, there was alarm in those dark eyes.

'Really?' Ibrahim responded. 'And you didn't say hello?' His question was polite and so too was her response, even if was a lie.

'I didn't actually see you.' She gave a vague wave of her hand as she lied. 'I just heard the steward saying that you were on board. I'm sorry if I was rude.'

'No need to apologise.' There was, Georgie was sure, a breath of relief in his voice. He even smiled again in her direction. 'Just make sure next time you say hello.'

The driver came up and had a brief word with Karim.

'What are we waiting for?' Felicity asked.

'Georgie's luggage has been loaded, but Ibrahim's is taking a while to come off.'

'*Lā Shy,*' Ibrahim said and Felicity, who must have picked up some of the language, frowned.

'You've got no luggage?'

'Just carry-on.' He held up a smart bag that Georgie was positive he hadn't been holding on boarding.

The car ride was short, the conversation seemingly pleasant, but it was mainly Georgie and Felicity speaking.

Back at the palace Ibrahim had an extremely cursory chat with his family, then excused himself with an outright lie.

'I couldn't sleep on the plane.'

When he left them, Georgie could relax a little and after Felicity had fed the baby, she was delighted to have a proper cuddle. 'She's stunning.' Georgie enthused again.

'Her lungs are!' Karim said. 'Half the palace was woken at four a.m. this morning.'

'I had the French windows open to let in some air.' Felicity grinned and Georgie could only marvel at the changes in her sister. She had always been so tense and uptight, but there was a lightness to her now. Her face glowed as she smiled up at her husband. 'Anyway, soon it won't just be Azizah disrupting the palace.'

'When is Jasmine's baby due?' Georgie asked.

'Jamal,' Felicity gently corrected her, because her sister found it impossible to keep up with all the names. 'She's got five weeks to go and I just can't wait.'

'Is that the aunt-to-be talking,' Georgie asked, 'or the midwife?'

'Both,' Felicity admitted. And as easily as that the conversation flowed.

Even if her sister was a princess now, even if she lived in a palace far away, she was still Felicity, still her big sister, still the person Georgie loved most in the world. Karim did have to dash off, but the girls hardly noticed, there was too much to catch up on. Long after they had eaten and late, late into the night, when everyone else was in bed, still the sisters sat talking in a sumptuous, surprisingly informal lounge at the front of the palace, the windows open and fragrant air drifting in. Felicity had the baby monitor by her side, and somehow Georgie found the words to tell her sister about a marriage that had happened more than three years ago, a marriage she had soon realised was a mistake.

'You're disappointed.' Georgie could tell.

'No.' Felicity shook her head. 'I don't know. I understand you felt you had to get away from home. I'm just sad you couldn't tell me.'

'I didn't feel I could tell anyone at the time.' Georgie admitted. 'I haven't told any of my friends. I just thought Mike… He seemed so solid, so mature…' She looked over at her sister. 'But it turned out he was a bully, like Dad—except he wore a suit and instead of beer it was expensive whisky. It only took a few weeks for me to come to my senses. I'm lucky…'

'Lucky?'

'A lot of women stay. I got out of it quickly. It just took a couple of years to face up to the paperwork and legalities and then another year of waiting. My divorce came through just as I was leaving for here. I'm finally free.'

'You've been free for ages,' Felicity said, but Georgie didn't try to explain her feelings to her sister. How some principle had held her back, how until her divorce was through she hadn't felt free to start dating, and in many ways it had been the healthiest thing for her—that time had taught her that she didn't need a man to escape to, or run to. Everything she needed, she possessed already.

'You won't tell Mum.'

'God, no!' Felicity's response was immediate. 'And

don't talk about it here, they just wouldn't understand at all.'

'Promise me that you won't tell anyone.' The intimate conversation was interrupted. Headlights flooded the lounge with light. The sound of a car unfamiliar to Georgie in the large grounds was followed by chatter and laughter and then the slam of a car door. There was the running of feet on the stone stairs and Felicity's lips tightened.

'He's so inconsiderate. It was the same last time he was here.' And when a wail came up over the intercom she pulled open the lounge door to address Ibrahim, who was talking loudly to a sleepy maid.

'You've woken Azizah.'

'Not necessarily.' So effortlessly he slipped from Arabic to English. 'I may be mistaken, but I'm sure I read somewhere that babies tend to wake in the night.'

Sarcasm suited him, it *so* suited him that Georgie let out a small giggle, but Ibrahim did not look at her. Instead he spoke to Felicity. 'I'm sorry if I woke her...I forgot there is now a baby in the palace.'

'There'll be two soon!' Felicity said. 'So you'd better start remembering.'

'No need. I'm flying back to London in a couple of days, before the palace turns into a crèche.' As Felicity headed off to tend to her baby, he acknowledged Georgie, his voice distinctly cool when he did. 'I was not expecting to see you here.' Ibrahim said. 'You never mentioned you were coming.'

'Neither did you,' Georgie pointed out.

'Your flight?' Ibrahim checked. 'How was it?' And something told her he was concerned that she *had* seen him, that she knew the sleek, poised man who had arrived in Zaraq had not been the man that left London, but Georgie chose not to tell.

'Wonderful.' Georgie said, but didn't elaborate, and Ibrahim said nothing to fill the stretch of silence, just walked across the lounge and sat on the sofa opposite as a maid brought in his drink. She didn't know what to say to him and he certainly wasn't giving her any help. Georgie was relieved when her sister called from the stairs. 'Georgie! Can you give me a hand with Azizah?'

'I'll say goodnight, then.' He didn't return the farewell, but she watched his jaw tighten when clearly she hadn't jumped quickly enough and Felicity called to her again. As she walked past, Ibrahim caught her wrist. 'That's what maids are for.' She looked down at his long fingers wrapped around her pale wrist and she wished he would drop the contact, wished he would not look up at her because her face was on fire. 'Tell her you are taking refreshments with me.'

'I'm happy to help my sister with Azizah.'

'At one in the morning?' Ibrahim said. 'Does she have you on call all night?' He watched her face burn, felt the hammer of her radial pulse beneath his fingers in response to his touch, and in that moment he could almost have forgiven her for rejecting him. He considered pulling her down onto his lap. 'Join me.' It wasn't a request, Georgie knew that—it was a challenge.

'I'm here to spend time with my sister and niece.' He dropped her wrist and without another word she left the room and walked through the maze of the palace to join Felicity in the nursery where she had settled down to feed.

'What kept you?' Felicity asked as Georgie closed the door.

'I was just talking to Ibrahim.' Georgie kept her voice light.

'Why?' And there was challenge too in Felicity's question, just a teeny call to arms, and Georgie refused to go there, choosing to tease instead.

'Why wouldn't I? It was either chat to a beautiful man or watch my sister breastfeed.'

To her credit, Felicity smiled.

'He asked about my flight. I just said goodnight.'

'Stay away from him,' Felicity warned. 'He's trouble. I've seen how he treats women—he'd eat you alive and then spit out the pips.'

'We were just saying goodnight!' Georgie laughed, but Felicity would not relent.

'He's so arrogant. Strolls back unannounced and expects everyone to jump to his whims, swans around the palace without a care in the world.' Georgie opened her mouth to interrupt because Ibrahim had looked far from carefree on the plane, but she decided against it, intuitively knowing Ibrahim wouldn't want that information shared. 'He's completely spoilt!' Felicity moaned on. 'Way too used to getting his own way, though not for much longer.'

'What do you mean?' Georgie asked, but Felicity shook her head.

'I've said too much.'

'It's me!' Georgie pointed out. 'And given what I told you earlier…'

'Okay,' Felicity relented, but, paranoid as ever, she had Georgie check and double-check that the intercom was turned off, then still spoke in a whisper. 'The king's had enough. Karim told me he's going to be talking to Ibrahim tomorrow. He wants him back in Zaraq, he's tired of his youngest son's ways. Ibrahim was supposed to go to London to study engineering and then come back, but he's finished his master's now and there's still no sign of him returning. Ibrahim's working mainly from there and saying that he wants to continue with his studies, but the king wants him here.'

'So, is he closing the open cheque book?' Georgie struggled to keep her voice light.

'He tried that a couple of years ago apparently.' Felicity sighed. 'And Ibrahim promptly went into business with one of Zaraq's leading architects. A lot of that dazzling skyline is thanks to my brother-in-law's brilliant brain. Ibrahim doesn't actually need royal financial support.'

'So how can he stop him?' Georgie asked. 'If Ibrahim doesn't want to be here, how can his father force him?'

'His father's king,' Felicity pointed out. 'And Ibrahim, at the end of the day, is a royal prince and privilege comes with responsibility.'

'You're starting to sound like them!' Georgie attempted a joke, but Felicity shook her head.

'Look at all the work Karim does for the people. He's out there now in the middle of the desert, working with sick people, while Ibrahim's working his way along the bar at the casino like a tourist. Well, Ibrahim's a prince and the king's tired of waiting for him to act like one.' Even though she was whispering, she still dropped her voice. 'He's going to be choosing a bride for him, whether he wants it or not. Soon Ibrahim's going to be coming home for good.'

CHAPTER FIVE

She'd slept too much on the plane and Georgie woke before sunrise, pulled the shutters open and properly surveyed her gorgeous room then climbed back into bed. After a moment's deliberation, she did what Felicity had told her to if she wanted anything, anything at all, and picked up the bedside phone. It didn't even ring once before it was answered, and in no time at all there was a tray laden with coffee and fruit and juices being delivered not just to her room but onto a bedside table. Her pillows were rearranged and Georgie cringed at the attention and wondered how Felicity could have so easily got used to it.

The coffee was too strong, too sweet and had an almost smoky flavour to it and she sipped it slowly, then chose to take her tray and enjoy the sight of the sun rising over the ocean.

Opening the French windows, she stepped out onto the balcony and watched the magical display—the sky lit up with pinks and oranges, the air warm on her skin. She was filled with a yearning to see a desert sunrise, to follow those warm fingers of light and see them awaken all that was behind. But as much as Georgie wanted to witness the splendour, she knew that again this trip it would be unlikely—Felicity was very busy and wouldn't want to leave little Azizah overnight.

One day she'd see it. Georgie told herself to be patient, but she was drawn to the magic Ibrahim had so readily dismissed, wanted to find out more for herself about the tales of the desert, to sample the food and inhale the oils, to see more of Zaraq than just the shops and the palace.

And then she saw him. A man on his horse. It could have been any of the brothers, from this distance it might even have been the king, but her heart told her it was Ibrahim. He certainly didn't look like a man who was recovering from the previous night's excess and not for the first time Georgie wondered if Felicity was mistaken about how Ibrahim spent his evenings. There was something about the speed of his riding, a combination of youth, vigor and power as he hurtled along the beach that told her it was him. He pulled up suddenly, patting the beast's neck and guiding him to a slow walk in the water, and then he looked up and saw the sun glisten on the palace and saw Georgie watching him.

He did not acknowledge her, did not lift a hand to wave. He just turned and kicked his horse back into a gallop, leaving a white streak of surf behind him, and she knew she'd just been snubbed. Still, you didn't say no to a man like Ibrahim and then expect a cheery wave the following morning.

Why was he here? Georgie wondered, as she showered

and dressed. What had suddenly prompted him to return unannounced? Oh, she'd seen him dashing and smiling, descending on Zaraq oozing charm and bearing gifts.

She'd seen the torment in his face too—only not even Ibrahim knew that.

The thought stayed with her as she showered and, dressed, joined her sister for breakfast.

'Is this okay?' she asked as she took her seat. It was a perpetual question for Georgie while in Zaraq. She was dressed in a loose-fitting cream shift dress with flat, strappy sandals and even though it was modest, she still felt as if she was showing way too much skin.

'Relax!' Felicity said. 'You look wonderful. It's only if you come out with me on official business, which you won't,' she hastily added when Georgie's eyes widened in horror, 'that you would have to cover up.' And then Felicity gave a wry laugh. 'Actually, technically you wouldn't. You're married after all.'

'Not any more.'

'Oh, but you are in Zaraq.' Felicity said, but didn't get to elaborate as the king came out to the courtyard where they were taking breakfast.

'Have you seen Ibrahim?' Felicity didn't turn a hair, but Georgie felt her heart pound because the king was a formidable man, especially close up, and he didn't look best pleased. 'No doubt he is still sleeping.' She wanted to correct him, to tell the king that Ibrahim was, in fact, out riding, but she knew it wasn't her place, even though the king sounded irritated. 'Where is everyone?'

'Karim left early to attend a meeting on the health

situation with the Bedouins,' Felicity answered calmly. 'I haven't seen anyone else.'

'Well, if you see Ibrahim, please remind him that I want him to come to my office before he no doubt disappears again.'

'Not likely.' Felicity said, once the King was safely out of earshot. 'I'm staying well out of their way today and so are you.' She smiled at her sister. 'We're off to the spa for the morning!'

It wasn't quite as simple as that. Felicity hadn't left Azizah for any length of time with Rina the nanny, and spent ages explaining to her about how her stored breast milk was to be used. She was still rather tense when she and Georgie climbed into the limousine.

'She'll be fine,' Georgie soothed. 'Rina seems wonderful with her.'

'I know.' Felicity admitted. 'I'm going to have to get used to leaving her—there are so many functions and I'm also thinking of going back to work! Just occasionally,' Felicity said, seeing Georgie's eyes widen. 'Midwifery is what I love, it's who I am, and I don't ever want to lose that. Rina is lovely and everything but Azizah doesn't seem to relax with her.' Georgie knew what was coming. They'd had this conversation so many times before and she tried to divert it.

'Maybe she needs a little more time—just her and Rina,' Georgie attempted. 'You do hover a bit. Rina seems wonderful, you just don't give her a chance. It's good you're out this morning.'

But Felicity would not relent. 'I want Azizah to grow

up with family.' She looked at Georgie. 'I want to be with my family too. Mum's considering it, but I know she'd jump if you were here too. Please, Georgie, say you'll seriously think about it.'

And it would be so easy to say yes, because she missed her sister and niece too. So very easy to give up trying to get her holistic healing business off the ground and just sink into the luxurious lifestyle her sister was offering.

Too easy.

Felicity had always looked out for her, had always looked after her through difficult times. The reason Felicity had first come to Zaraq had been to pay off the loan she had taken out to pay for Georgie's rehab, and though the offer was tempting, there was a need in Georgie to go it alone, to prove to herself she could get by without her big sister's help.

'Let's talk about it another time.' Georgie said as the car headed off and she craned her neck for a glimpse as the palace gates slid open.

'What are you looking at?'

'Just the view.' Georgie smiled. 'I can't believe I'm staying in a palace.'

'You could live in a palace.' Felicity pushed, but Georgie just gave a noncommittal smile, her mind elsewhere.

It wasn't the palace, she had been trying to get a glimpse of.

It had been Ibrahim.

It was always Ibrahim, not that she could admit it to

her sister. And he stayed on her mind as they arrived in Zaraqua and an external glass elevator propelled them to the forty-second floor of a skyscraper, and Georgie remembered that she didn't like heights.

'Ibrahim's work!' Felicity said to Georgie's pale face as they shot skyward. 'He designed this lift.'

'Then remind me to tell him I hate him!' Georgie shivered. 'And tell me when I can open my eyes.'

'Now.'

They stepped into spa heaven. The lights were dimmed and the air fragrant as they were led to a changing room that was twice the size of Georgie's small flat at home. 'I want to try everything…' Georgie said as she changed into a gown, her mind exploding with ideas for her fledgling business back home. 'Is there a menu?'

'It's all sorted,' Felicity said. 'We're here for the Hamman Ritual and there isn't a single decision you have to make. It's absolute bliss.'

It was.

Through dimmed rooms lit with candles they were led, and as Georgie's eyes adjusted she saw the tadelakt wall with its intricate tiling.

'It's so hot,' Georgie whispered.

'You'll get used to it.'

Oh, she'd love to get used to it. She was lowered into a sunken bath and her body washed with black soap and then, on emerging, she was led to another heated room where every inch of her skin was exfoliated, the bathing repeated and then every superfluous hair removed with sugar and honey. From heated room to heated room they were guided, every treatment skillfully applied, every scent thoughtfully chosen, and two hours later, wrapped in a robe, sipping at fragrant tea and enjoying the soft music, Georgie smiled back at her sister, who was watching her.

'I can't believe how far you've come.'

'I know.' Georgie admitted, closing her eyes and letting joy flood through her, because a couple of years ago today would have been impossible, the thought of a spa abhorrent, but now she could relax, could enjoy healing hands on her, and it was her dream to in some small way impart the same experience in her work. She wanted to help others as she had been helped.

'Your Highness!' Georgie had forgotten for a moment her sister was now a princess and she was jerked out of her introspection as a nervous receptionist approached. 'We would, of course, never normally disturb you, it is a strict rule of the spa, but the palace has called…'

'It's fine,' Felicity said, and took the phone and then spoke with a nail technician, who was standing by. 'Would you excuse us, please?' Only when they were alone did she take the call, a smile on her face as she listened, her voice reassuring when she spoke. 'No, you're not making a fuss…I'll come now.' She paused for a moment. 'You were right to call me.'

'What's going on?'

'Jamal,' Felicity said. 'She's done this a couple of times. Hassan's away and she's anxious, she's not sure whether or not she's having contractions.'

'Surely there are a million doctors on call for her?'

'Exactly.' Felicity rolled her eyes. 'The whole country is holding their breath about this baby and the palace doctor isn't taking a single chance—last week she ended up being taken to hospital and monitored. There were the press waiting before she even arrived at the hospital and it was only Braxton-Hicks' contractions. She probably doesn't want another repeat.'

'Poor thing.'

'You stay here and finish. If we both dash off, they'll suspect something,' Felicity said. 'I don't want to give anyone here a hint—I'll make out that Azizah's fretting for me or something.'

Georgie stayed for a little while, had her feet hennaed with pretty flowers and her toenails painted, but it wasn't as much fun without Felicity and after an hour or so Georgie chose to head for home, or rather the palace that she called home for now. Even as the car swept into the driveway, still she had trouble believing this was where her sister actually lived. It was just a world away from the small house in which they had grown up, in the North of England. A house Georgie had never considered home. A house she had run away from at every opportunity.

For the first time the palace doors didn't magically part as Georgie climbed the steps, but just as she was wondering if such a magnificent door even *had* a doorbell, it opened, and there, most unexpectedly, was Ibrahim.

'Where's Felicity?' She peered over his shoulder as he let her in.

'At the hospital,' he replied. As she stood in the hall-way two maids dashed up the stairs without stopping to greet her or bow their heads to Ibrahim. 'Jamal is having the baby, so things have been thrown into chaos here—they are trying to get hold of Hassan.'

'I thought it was a false alarm. It's too soon!' Georgie said, but Ibrahim seemed unperturbed.

'Your sister says it is a little early, but it will be just fine. My father just left for the hospital. Felicity explained you were at the spa. She was going to have a message sent for you but things started to move rather quickly, otherwise I'm sure we would not have been left alone.' And that small comment told her he had been warned about her, but he did not linger on the matter, just stood silently as a group of robed man swept past, all deep in urgent conversation.

'Where's Azizah?'

'With the nanny. She is getting her ready.' At first she assumed it was a slight slip in English, that the nanny was changing a nappy or getting her niece dressed, but Georgie soon realised there had been no miscommunication.

'She will bring her to the car. You need to get your things together too. We should leave soon,' he said, but Georgie just stood there.

'Leave?'

'We need to get to the hospital.'

'Me?'

'You're family,' Ibrahim said. 'And the future king

is about to be born. Why wouldn't you want to be there?'

'Because I've never spoken to my sister's sister-in-law before for starters!'

Felicity had warned her to hold her tongue, to think before she spoke, and Georgie wondered if she'd gone too far, but his mouth moved into a smile she hadn't been privy to in a very long time, a smile like no other because it told her that his question had been teasing, that he took no offence at her response. It was a smile that welcomed her to his world, that told her he understood how bizarre this all must seem. Then he must have remembered he was still sulking because his smile faded and his words were stern when they came.

'I am looking forward to this about as much as you are. There is no choice.'

Rina came down with little Azizah, who was wrapped in a delicate cream shawl ready to meet her new cousin, and the enormity of what lay ahead hit Georgie then.

'I really don't think anyone would notice if I didn't attend.'

'Oh, they'd notice.' Ibrahim said. 'You are to bring Azizah.'

'I'm not ready…' She gestured to her clothing. The loose white dress was crumpled from the oils, her hair heavy and greasy from her scalp massage, and she didn't have a scrap of make-up on. Worse was the thought of being amongst the royals. Being a part of such a prestigious event had her head in a spin—but a maid slithered a veil over her and Georgie was grateful in that moment for the robes, for the shield, for the anonymity it would afford her.

Without it, she would never have made it through the day.

As they all walked out to the waiting car and she saw the police motorbike escorts waiting for them, it was all too intense for Georgie. The silver limousine with blacked-out windows that had taken Felicity and herself to the day spa had been replaced by a black vehicle that was far more formal. There was even a flag at the front.

'It's like a royal parade,' Georgie attempted as the door opened, and then she swallowed at Ibrahim's response.

'That's exactly what it is.'

One minute she was enjoying a spa day with her sister, the next she was to be a visible member of Zaraq's most prominent family. One minute she was an occasional, albeit enthusiastic aunt. Now, though, when Rina handed her Azizah, she carried in her arms Zaraq's newest princess.

'Why aren't the windows blacked out?'

'We are on official duty!' Ibrahim informed her. 'The people of Zaraq want to see their royal family on a day like today.'

Perhaps he mistook her panicked eyes. 'We can go separately if you prefer,' Ibrahim offered, but it wasn't being with him that had Georgie nervous, it was the thought of doing this without her sister.

'No,' Georgie croaked. 'Stay.'

She was a complicated mix, Ibrahim thought as he climbed in beside her. So outwardly confident, so bold and assured, and yet… He looked over, but she stared ahead, her blue eyes unblinking, and he could hear her drawing in deep breaths. There was a fragility to her that his brother missed, that others missed, and he could not just abandon her on a day like today. As the car moved from the palace and into the streets, Ibrahim told her a little of what she could expect.

'Now that the king has arrived at the hospital, there will be great excitement, people gathering.'

It was all more than Georgie could immediately take in, though later she would surely go over it in her mind again and again, for as they approached the hospital, crowds of people were waving and cheering as the latest royal car arrived. It was the most bizarre moment of her life, and as she climbed out, holding Azizah, never had Georgie felt more responsible. She was filled with a need to take care of her niece as Felicity would want her to. She held Azizah close and pulled the shawl to shield the baby's eyes from the fierce afternoon sun. Ibrahim waited patiently and then walked beside her, greeting waiting staff members who briefed him as they went to join the rest of the royals.

'It won't be long apparently,' Ibrahim informed her. 'The birth is imminent, and Hassan has just arrived.'

They arrived at a waiting room like no other. There were staff on hand offering refreshments, and Rina, who had followed in another car, offered to take Azizah, but

Georgie declined. 'I'll hold her. Where's my sister?' she asked, and it was Ibrahim who found out.

'Felicity is staying with Jamal for the birth.' He saw her blue eyes shutter. 'I know it's a bit overwhelming.'

'A bit?'

'Very,' Ibrahim conceded. 'I will stay with you.' Even if it had been forbidden by his brother—in fact, just that morning, as Ibrahim had been heading out for a ride, Karim had issued an updated warning for him to stay away from Georgie—he did not care. The ways of his family overwhelmed even Ibrahim at times, so how much harder must it be for Georgie? And without the help of her sister too. 'You don't have to worry about anything.'

Georgie blew out a breath. 'I don't know how Felicity copes...'

'It's the life she has chosen, though it's not like this all the time' He watched as she held little Azizah closer, more, he guessed, for her own sake than the baby's.

'Well, I couldn't do it.'

'She does very well.'

She frowned as she turned to him, surprised by the genuine admiration in his voice when he referred to Felicity. 'I thought you didn't like her.'

'I like her a lot,' Ibrahim said. 'My concern is for you.' And then he gave a wry smile. 'Not that you want it.'

'She's not using me.'

'Of course she is,' Ibrahim said. 'And I don't blame her a bit for it. She is here alone in a foreign country, she wants her family close—and she wants you to use her too.' He'd voiced every one of her thoughts. 'She wants you, the sister she loves, to share in the riches, but you feel beholden.'

And she closed her eyes, so raw was that nerve.

'Look after yourself, Georgie.'

'Like you do?'

He was about to say, yes, give his usual arrogant reply, yet she made him think, made him pause, and rather than answer her question, he looked at his niece, sleeping the sleep of the innocent. He ran a finger down the baby's cheek and his reply was honest.

'Like I try to.' Ibrahim said, 'but we are all beholden.'

For now, circumstance dictated he be here for the royal birth. It was his duty to see it through, yet he was surprised at his building anticipation. He had been touched by the people's joy as they had driven through the streets. He was relieved perhaps because, when his father had been ill, when Hassan and Jamal had failed to produce a baby, there had been talk of Hassan renouncing his birthright, which would have bought Ibrahim one step closer to the unthinkable—that he might one day be king.

He was relieved, that was all, Ibrahim told himself as the lusty cries of a newborn assured Zaraq's future.

'A son!' The king beamed. 'Our future king has been born. A little small, a little weak, but the doctor assures us he is healthy, that he will grow and be strong.' He looked over at his errant youngest son and in a rare tactile moment embraced him. 'It is good you are here to share in this day.'

It felt good.

The unvoiced admission surprised him.

'Come,' the king ordered. 'We move to the balcony to share the joyous news with our people.'

It was a good day, an exciting day, a miraculous day. Ibrahim looked at Georgie, who was completely out of her depth and more than a little lost, and as he went to her side he could see the terror in her eyes. As promised, he stood by her as they moved to the balcony.

'This,' he explained, 'is the announcement. This tells our people all is well. When Hassan and Jamal's first son, Kaliq, was born and we knew he would not survive, there was a small press release and no further comment. Today the people of Zaraq will know all is well.'

She stepped onto the balcony, holding her tiny niece, and heard the screams and cheers from the streets below.

'You're doing great.' He was being incredibly nice.

'Thanks.' Georgie shivered through her teeth. 'The thing is I have no idea what it is I'm doing.' Still, the excitement was palpable and Georgie joined in, even waved to the people below and had an 'if only they knew' moment when she thought of her friends back home. 'Luckily it's just for today.'

But it wasn't just one day for Ibrahim. This was what he was being asked to return to, he thought as he stared out at the crowd. This might be his future.

CHAPTER SIX

'Do I have to wear this?' This was so not what Georgie had come to Zaraq for. It was a trip to see her sister, to spend time with her niece, but now she was to dine tonight with the princes and the king, and it seemed there was no getting around it.

'The heir was born today.' She could hear the exasperation and guilt in her sister's voice. 'Georgie, we will have time together, it's just with Jamal's baby coming early... Please, just go with things for a couple of days.'

It was arguably worse than the wedding. To ensure she was fit for the king's table, maids had braided her long blonde hair and kohled her eyes, and now a garment had been laid out on her bed—a long lemon dress with beading and patterns down two front panels. It wasn't even close to anything she would have chosen.

'You look gorgeous,' Felicity lied, because the lemon would have looked stunning with olive skin and a coil of dark hair, but it clashed with blonde and both sisters knew it.

'I look like a lemon meringue pie.' Georgie responded,

but she didn't want to add to her sister's guilt. She actually managed a laugh as she peered in the mirror. 'And why is my rouge orange? Anyway, it doesn't matter, it's just dinner…I'll be fine. You will be sitting next to me?' Georgie checked, but her heart tripped to a race when Felicity grimaced.

'I will, but I might have to pop up and feed Azizah. She fell asleep straight after her bath so I don't think she's going to last the whole meal.'

'You can't leave me with them.'

'I wouldn't normally—who could know Jamal was going to have the baby early? And I didn't know there'd be a formal function the day he was born.'

'Formal!' Georgie gulped.

'Well, not formal exactly,' Felicity quickly backtracked. 'I mean, it's family but Jamal's family are coming too and they're very traditional…Georgie, I don't want Rina to feed Azizah unless I really can't be there. I have had to stand my ground with this—it's the height of bad manners here to excuse yourself during a meal, but Karim's spoken to his father…'

'You've got an exemption.'

'I can't back down.' Felicity was torn. 'But if it is too much for you… If it's going to set you back…'

'Felicity.' Georgie was firm. 'Not everything goes back to my eating disorder. Any person would be nervous at having to attend a formal dinner with a king.'

'I know. I'm just so sorry that it's on your second night. It won't happen again. We don't usually dine with the king—normally it's Karim and me in our suite.'

'So who's going to be there?'

'The king, and Hassan will be there with Jamal's parents and family. Ibrahim, I hope.'

'Hope?' Georgie closed her eyes for a moment. She really did not want to face him looking like this.

'That's all you can do when he's around.' Felicity gave a wry smile. 'How was he today?'

'He seemed to enjoy the celebration—he was thrilled for his brother.'

'Karim said you two spent a lot of time together.'

'He speaks English,' Georgie said tersely. She did not have to explain herself, they had done nothing wrong, but she quickly changed the subject. 'What about the queen?'

'You know she doesn't live here.'

'So when will she get to see her grandson?'

'When Hassan and Jamal take him to see her—like I did when Azizah was born. Mind you, with him being a little bit premature, it might not be for a while.'

'So she won't get to see him?'

'Georgie, please…' Her sister was nervous and it irritated Georgie.

'We're not allowed to talk about it even in the privacy of my bedroom?' Georgie shook her head in disbelief. 'I don't know how you live like this, Felicity.'

'I have a wonderful life,' Felicity said, 'and of course we can talk about things. It's just…' Felicity screwed her eyes closed for a second. 'Just not at dinner. Georgie, I'm asking you to be discreet. There are things that aren't to be discussed.' She tried for the umpteenth time to explain to her younger sister the strange ways of Zaraq. 'It's a very delicate subject, The king misses her terribly, he mourns for her.'

'She's not dead,' Georgie pointed out. 'All he has to do is pick up the phone.' She rolled her eyes. 'Don't worry, I'm not going to say anything to embarrass you— I'll be suitably demure.'

She was, and it had nothing to do with Felicity's warning. The vast table, the company, the introductions, the surroundings had Georgie overwhelmed.

There was no sign of Ibrahim and she heard the king say his name a couple of times to Karim.

'When do we eat?' Georgie asked her sister, when they had been sitting for what seemed ages.

'When the prodigal son appears.' Felicity answered, and Georgie felt nervous on his behalf. 'Are you okay?'

'I'm fine.' But even if she appeared calm, inwardly she was dreading that her sister might have to leave. Especially as Felicity had told her that though they usually did their best to converse in English when she was around, it wasn't possible tonight as Jamal's family spoke only Arabic. 'They are discussing when a photo of the new heir will be released.' Felicity did her best to keep up with the conversation, but even that lifeline was lost when a maid whispered in her ear and Felicity, with a rather terse nod from the king, excused herself.

It was interminable, smiling and laughing and nodding when the others did, though Georgie had no idea what was being said. She actually found herself wishing they'd bring the food out, just to give her something to do. But then, like a summer shower on a stifling day, Ibrahim strolled in and all Georgie could wonder was how he got away with wearing Western clothes—he was in black dinner trousers and a slim-fitting white shirt and she wondered if he'd been out riding and had just pulled some clothes on, because his hair was tousled and he hadn't bothered with shaving.

'You are late.' The king was less than impressed. The conversation was in English now, no doubt to avoid any embarrassment in front of the esteemed guests.

'I had to make a phone call,' Ibrahim said without apology.

'It is dinner,' the king said.

'With family.' Ibrahim's smile was black as he made his point. 'Surely we can relax and share in such a fine occasion.' He slid into the empty seat beside Georgie.

'Felicity is sitting there.' Karim's response was immediate.

'Where is she, then?'

'Feeding Azizah.'

'She left you to deal with this lot?' Ibrahim looked less than impressed and just shrugged as Karim frowned at him. 'I'll sit with you till she gets back.' He switched back to Arabic then and spoke for a moment or two with the guests and then turned his attention back to Georgie.

'You look…' His eyes drifted down and then back to her face, and there was a hint of a tease in his smile. 'Like you did the day I met you.'

'Ah, yes,' Georgie said, remembering the apricot bridesmaid's dress. 'I don't think the maids are used to dressing blondes.' She winked. 'I'll have to have a little word.'

He was wonderful company. She even forgot to be nervous for a little while, forgot, if it was possible to, just how attracted she was to him. She was just herself with him that night, and that was all she needed to be.

'I thought they'd be serving now that you are here,' Georgie commented when, despite Felicity's prediction, it seemed that the dreaded meal was taking for ever to come out.

'It shouldn't be too much longer,' Ibrahim explained, 'Most of the socialising is done before dinner. Once it gets to coffee, the evening is over.'

'Really?' Georgie gave a tight smile in Karim's direction. 'My sister never said.'

Still, when the first course was finally served, somehow he must have sensed the small lick of hers lips wasn't borne of anticipation as a stream of maids approached with dishes.

'You'll be fine.' He watched as she politely nodded, but he could see the nervousness in her eyes. 'You really will.'

'I read that it's rude not to clear your plate.' Georgie was almost breathless at the admission, but without Felicity beside her, the prospect of dining in such plush surroundings with food she was unfamiliar with was becoming increasingly daunting.

'It's mezze,' he said, 'just the starter—dips, pastries

and pickles…' He explained the lavish spread. 'Just take a little and if you like it, go back for more. Excuse me a moment,' he said, and turned his attention to his father. '*Bekra*,' came his brief response, then he turned back to Felicity. 'My father is asking when I am going to the hospital again. I said tomorrow.'

Somehow she relaxed, so much so she barely noticed when Felicity returned and after a brief awkward moment Ibrahim moved to the other side of the table.

'I'm so sorry.' Felicity said in a low voice. 'Georgie, I really am—'

'It's fine,' Georgie said. 'Honestly. Ibrahim's been wonderful.' She saw her sister's lips tighten, saw Felicity's worried blink as she glanced briefly at her brother-in-law and then back to Georgie.

'What?' Georgie frowned.

'Nothing,' Felicity said, but Georgie could tell she was rattled.

Ibrahim's behavior was impeccable. As the endless courses were served he spoke with the guests but he still carried on talking to Georgie, guiding her through the courses whenever Felicity was drawn into the main conversation.

As they ate their dessert—*mahlabia*, Ibrahim informed her from across the table, a creamy pudding layered with rose water—again she felt Felicity tense. Her sister's reaction incensed Georgie. Admittedly, thorough no fault of her own, Felicity had left her to her own devices all day, and Georgie shuddered to think how the day would have been without Ibrahim's guidance. Now

Felicity seemed annoyed that the two of them seemed to be getting on, even nudging Georgie when she laughed at something Ibrahim said.

'What?' Georgie asked. 'What have I done wrong now?'

'I'll talk to you later.'

She would be talking too.

Oh, yes, she'd say something, but later and when they were alone.

Coffee was served and, as Ibrahim had predicted, the evening ended. As farewells were said to Jamal's family, Hassan declared he would now return to the hospital to spend the first night with his wife and new son. But it would seem the evening was not quite over, for the king accepted another coffee and small biscuits were served. Just when everyone should be able to relax a touch more, the king frowned in annoyance as Ibrahim's phone rang loudly.

'Excuse me.' He stood as he answered it. 'I have to take this call.'

It was clearly the height of rudeness, and the conversation was strained as Ibrahim took his time. The king's face was like thunder as the minutes stretched on, and even Georgie was nervous as to what might happen when almost half an hour later an unrepentant Ibrahim returned to the room.

'What?' He glanced up at the silence and boldly addressed it.

'I will speak with you later.'

'Speak with me now,' Ibrahim said.

'You have kept the table waiting for the second time in one meal.'

'I told you to carry on.'

'We celebrate *as* a family.'

'Not quite.'

It wasn't indiscretions from Georgie they had to worry about. There was a dangerous edge to Ibrahim, a challenge in his stance as he took his place at the table and clicked his fingers. 'I would like champagne…' he glanced at his father '…to celebrate the birth of Zaraq's future king.'

There had been champagne at her sister's wedding, but only for visitors, and clearly it was not expected tonight, for the servant hesitated until a tense nod came from the king. 'Will anyone join me?' Ibrahim asked. Gorgeous black eyes swept the table and then met hers.

'No, thank you.' She could almost hear the sigh of relief from her sister as she declined his offer and everyone else at the table did the same.

'Not *quite* a family celebration.' Ibrahim picked up the conversation once his champagne was poured, and Georgie realised he wasn't just ignoring his father's anger, he was provoking it. 'Did not one of you think to call her?' Ibrahim's eyes roamed to his brother and then to his father. 'That is why I was late for dinner. I called my mother, naturally expecting her to already know the news…that this morning she became a grandmother.'

'Ibrahim,' Karim broke in. 'Not here.'

'Where, then?' Ibrahim said. 'This is family, is it not? Where do we discuss such things if not at dinner?'

'Tonight is a celebration,' the king said, though a muscle flickered in his cheek. 'I was going to have my secretary ring—'

'Your secretary?' Ibrahim sneered. 'Is that the same one who rang her when her son died? The same one who rang her when Hassan and Jamal's firstborn died? You know how her heart broke.'

'I had not spoken to your mother in years then.'

'But you're talking to her now,' Ibrahim said. 'You're more than talking with her, you're...' He stopped and collected himself then carried on. 'Could you not have rung today to make her heart soar?' His disgust was evident.

'You did not ring,' the king said.

'I thought you had!' Ibrahim would not back down. 'I assumed her husband had, given you are talking now, and that you were in London two weeks ago on *business*.'

'Silence.'

'That call I just took was from your wife,' Ibrahim sneered, 'my mother, our queen. The news I gave to her before dinner has just sunk in, now she is crying, sobbing, that she cannot see the future heir till Hassan can fit in a visit. She begs me to celebrate for her, to give him a kiss from the grandmother who cannot be here. She has poured champagne back in London and is raising a glass—I told her that I would do the same.'

His eyes scanned the table. 'Will anyone join my mother and me?'

There were no takers.

Karim shook his head, as did Felicity, and Georgie wanted to shake her.

'Georgie?' he offered, and she was beyond tempted to say yes this time, not for the drink but for the point he was making. But she refused to partake in a battle that was not hers, to play a game when she was not privy to the rules. She could hear the pain behind his statements, feel the injustice on his mother's behalf, but she was here with her sister, here to support her, not make trouble for her. Still, there was regret in her heart when again she declined.

'No, thank you.' She licked suddenly dry lips and dropped her gaze, but not before she saw a flash of disappointment in his eyes.

The king was not about to bend to his son.

'Tomorrow.' He rose from the table and immediately Karim stood and so too did Felicity. At her sister's nudge, Georgie followed. Only Ibrahim sat, not for long but there was reluctance, insolence even as rather too slowly he also stood. It did not go unnoticed. 'You will be in my study at eight a.m. Tomorrow, Ibrahim, you will listen to what I have to say.'

The door closed behind him but the tension did not leave the room.

'Why tonight, Ibrahim?' Karim challenged. 'Why did you have to spoil it?'

'Spoil it?' Ibrahim did not understand his brother,

his brother who would have been the king's choice as heir, a brother who had not even cried when his mother had left them. 'You mean voice it.'

'I mean, you make trouble whenever you return. There was no reason for this display.'

'No reason?' Ibrahim looked at his brother and then at Felicity. 'Imagine, years from now, Felicity, if it was Azizah who had delivered a child while you were on the other side of the world and Karim did not think even to call you.' He picked up the bottle and left them alone and Georgie fought the urge to follow him.

'He has a point.' Felicity turned to her husband. 'A very good one, in fact. You should have called her.' When Karim didn't answer, Felicity pushed on. 'We need to arrange a trip home.'

'We've been,' Karim said. 'We took Azizah home to meet your family and my mother when she was born.'

'Well, arrange another one,' Felicity said. 'I want Azizah to know all her family.'

'I'll sort it.' Karim stood. 'I'll go and speak to my father now. See how he is.'

But any magnanimous feelings Felicity had towards her brother-in-law were fleeting. 'Bloody Ibrahim,' Felicity shrilled when they were safe in her suite. 'He does this every time he's home.'

'As you said, he had a good point.'

'Well, of course you'd jump in on his side.' Felicity was pacing. 'Will you just stay away from him?'

'Why should I?' Georgie challenged. 'When he's the

only person whose been there for me all day. Am I not supposed to speak to him?'

'Of course you can speak to people—it's the little private conversations, the laughing at each other's jokes…' Felicity was having difficulty keeping her voice even and then she said it, just came right out and said what had been obvious to everyone. 'You two were flirting all night.'

'No!' Adamantly Georgie shook her head. 'We were talking. We were just talking…' Except that wasn't true. It had been his black eyes she had sought, his smile, his voice that had summoned her senses, and she couldn't blame her sister for noticing. 'I wasn't deliberately flirting.'

'You were the same at the wedding,' Felicity said. 'I know he's attractive and I know women don't stand a chance when he turns on the charm, but not here, Georgie, not in Zaraq, not with my husband's family. You can do what you like in London.'

'What's that supposed to mean?' Felicity always did this—made out she was some wild child, some perpetual problem to be dealt with.

'Just…' Felicity ran a hand thorough her hair. 'Let's just leave it, please, Georgie.'

'Leave what?' Georgie said.

'Nothing.' Felicity shook her head. 'I don't want to argue.' She gave a weak smile. 'I'm overreacting. It's been a long day and not just with Jamal. Karim's worried about the Bedouins, he's speaking with his father to try and sort out what to do. I've felt guilty all day for leaving you and it *was* good of Ibrahim to take you under his wing. I'm just tired, overreacting.'

'Go to bed,' Georgie said. 'You'll be up for Azizah in a couple of hours.' She saw Felicity's face pale just at the thought of it. 'Why don't you let Rina get up to her tonight?'

'Not you too!' Felicity was close to tears. 'I don't want Rina.'

'I can get up if you want,' Georgie said. 'You look exhausted.'

'You don't have to.'

'I want to,' Georgie said, and before Felicity could jump in, she did. 'I know she's to have your milk, but there's a whole freezer full. I'll take the intercom and you get some sleep and we'll have a nice day tomorrow.' She watched as Felicity nibbled on her lip. Clearly there were more duties she had to perform. 'Or the next day. It's not your fault the future king was born the day after I arrived.'

'You do understand?'

'I do,' Georgie lied, because she couldn't really believe everything her sister had married into. There were unspoken rules everywhere and no matter how she tried she seemed to put a foot wrong.

As she walked back to her bedroom she saw him standing on the balcony, looking out to the desert he loathed. He didn't turn round but she knew he had heard her because she saw his shoulders stiffen. She stood for a moment, wondering if he'd acknowledge her, wondering what she'd do if he did, but Ibrahim just poured another drink and deliberately ignored her.

'I can manage, thanks.' Felicity smiled at the maid in her bedroom, who was there to help her undress, and she blew out a breath when finally she was alone.

She should have said yes to him tonight.

There were a thousand ways she could justify not doing so. As she pulled out her hair, she thought of a few—she was here for her sister after all, it would have been disrespectful to the king…Georgie slipped off her shoes, undid the buttons on her dress and then took off the horrible rouge and kohl, slathered on some face cream and rubbed more melissa on her temples, telling herself she'd done the right thing, but her heart wasn't in it.

After brushing her teeth, she rinsed her mouth then poured the water down the sink. She looked into the mirror and could justify no more.

Taking the glass, she picked up the intercom and walked out through her suite and into the hallway to where he stood on the balcony. He didn't turn to greet her and she hadn't expected him to.

'I'm sorry.' But Ibrahim shook his head. 'I'm trying to apologise.'

'Well, you don't have to.' Finally he turned and filled her glass. 'I should not have put you in that situation.' The most difficult, complicated man she had ever met looked into her eyes and she wished that she could read what was in his. 'You are not beholden to me.' Always he surprised her. 'But, Georgie…' he glanced down at the intercom '…neither are you to your sister.'

'I'm just looking after my niece for the night.'

'I'm not just talking about that—there is tension between the two of you.'

'We love each other.'

'I know you do,' Ibrahim said. 'But there is…' He could not quite identify it. 'You hold back and so does she.'

'You're wrong.'

'Maybe,' Ibrahim admitted. 'But sometimes a row can be good. Sometimes the air needs to be cleared. You feel you are beholden?' he asked. 'That you owe something to her?' And his voice for the first time ever was tender, and there was both guilt and relief as she nodded, being more honest with another person than she had been in her life. Georgie rarely cried, and only really for physical pain but she hadn't fallen over in a long time. But just as he had at the nightclub, Ibrahim brought her near tears with just a few words.

'That's not good, Georgie.' He knew her from the inside; he pulled out her demons and told her to banish them. For a moment she wanted to run.

'She's helped me so much, though.'

'Have you thanked her?'

'Of course.'

'Did you mean it?'

She nodded.

'Then you're done,' Ibrahim said, except it surely

wasn't that simple. 'Lose the guilt, Georgie…' he smiled '…and come to bed with me instead.

'That last bit was a joke,' he added, then it wasn't his smile but the swallow beneath that told her something else—that he was remembering. For the first time in months he moved closer into her space and there was an almost imperceptible tightening to his nostrils, but to Georgie it was magnified tenfold, for she knew he was drawing in her scent as he lowered his head.

'Bal-smin.' He inhaled the fragrant air that swirled between them and she wondered if he would kiss her, could hardly hold onto her breath as she tried to keep speaking normally.

'We call it melissa…' And then there was no hope of speaking because his breath was on her cheek.

She thought he might kiss her, so badly she wanted to taste him again, she thought he might pull her just a little further in, but all he did was torment her with a slow appraisal that made her feel faint. He breathed in her scent, though he did not touch her physically, but to have him so close made her feel weak and, whatever his assessment, he was right to assume he could kiss her; he could touch her; he could have her right here on the balcony, and that, Georgie thought in a brief moment of clarity, was a very good reason to say goodnight.

'I've got to go,' she croaked.

'Then go now,' Ibrahim warned, which was wise.

She took the baby monitor from the ledge, walked to her room and made herself, forced herself, not to turn round, but there was little sanctuary in her bedroom.

She took off her dress and lay naked between cool sheets, knowing there was just one door between them and wondering if he'd pursue her—already she knew what her response would be.

But he didn't.

He left her burning, aroused and inflamed as once she had left him, as perhaps was his intention, Georgie realised. Maybe he did want her on her knees, begging, just so he could decline.

Thank God for the baby monitor.

An electronic chastity belt that blinked through the night and made lots of noise, and, far from resent it, Georgie was grateful to have it by her side.

For without it she'd have roamed the palace, looking for his door.

CHAPTER SEVEN

'You wanted to see me.' Ibrahim strode into the king's plush office ten minutes early. Yesterday's reprieve from his father had come more as an irritation than a relief to Ibrahim. He did not avoid things and though he wasn't looking forward to this conversation, he would rather it was over.

That he state his case and move on.

'Have a seat.' The king's voice was tired rather than assertive, which was unusual, but what came next was a complete surprise. He had expected to be met with a tirade, a challenge, but it was the father, not the ruler who met his eyes. 'You were right.'

'I'm always right.' Ibrahim smiled, perhaps the only one of the sons who dared and sometimes could get away with cheeking his father. 'Can I ask about what?'

'I should have informed your mother.' The smile faded from Ibrahim's face as his father continued. 'She deserved better than to hear it from her son, or the news, or my secretary.'

She deserved better, full stop, Ibrahim wanted to add, but knew better than to push it.

'She would not come to the phone this morning to accept my apology, so I am heading there to deliver it in person.'

'You are leaving Zaraq now?' It was almost unthinkable. The streets were awash with celebration, this was Zaraq's greatest day, and his father was leaving?

'I will be home in time for his discharge from hospital and I will visit the baby this morning. The people do not necessarily have to know. And if they do find out…' The king gave a dismissive shrug. 'I am visiting my wife to share in person the joyous news.' He looked at his son, at the youngest but the deepest, the one, out of all of them, he could read the least. 'You don't look pleased.'

'Why would I be?'

'Since my illness I have been going to London more often. Your brothers are pleased to see your mother and I getting on…but not you.'

'No.' Ibrahim was honest, to his detriment at times, but he was always honest. 'I don't like my mother being treated as a tart.'

'Ibrahim.' There was a roar that would surely have woken Azizah, but Ibrahim didn't even flinch. 'Never speak of her like that.'

'That is what you make her,' Ibrahim said. 'For years you ignored her.'

'I housed her, she had an allowance.'

'Now you lavish her with gifts, fly over there when you are able…' He lifted his hands and danced them like a puppeteer and just sat as his father came round the table and raised his fist to him. 'Go ahead,' Ibrahim said, 'but it won't silence me—it never has before.' As his father dropped his fist, Ibrahim continued his tirade. 'You expect her to be home, to drop everything when you deign to come over, yet at important times, at family times, she cannot be present—what would you call her then?'

'I don't need your approval.'

'That is good,' Ibrahim said, 'because you will never get it.' He stood and his father ordered him to sit.

'I would prefer to stand.'

'I did not dismiss you. There is more to discuss.'

'As I said, I would prefer to stand.'

'Then so too will I,' the king said, and he stood and faced his youngest. There was challenge in the air and neither would back away from it. 'I have been patient,' the king said. 'More than patient. But that patience is now running out. You are needed here.'

'I am needed there,' Ibrahim retorted. 'Or will you only be happy when she is completely alone—will her punishment be sufficient when all her children are here in Zaraq?'

'This isn't about your mother. This is about you and your duty to Zaraq.' Ibrahim refused to listen. He turned to go but his father's words followed him. 'Your place is here—you can run, but the desert will call you, I know that it *is* calling you.'

Ibrahim laughed in his face. 'I cannot stand the desert.'

'You fear it,' his father taunted. 'I see you ride along

the beaches and along the outskirts, but this time home you have not been in. If you choose not to listen to that call, then you will listen to me. I am selecting a bride—'

'I can make my own choices.'

'You never make wise ones, though,' the king said to his son's departing back.

He wanted to leave and he would, Ibrahim decided, just as soon as his father had gone—he did not care to share a flight with his father. He wanted no more of this land, of its rules, and he would not have his wife chosen for him.

He had been right to come back, Ibrahim realised. It reminded him how he could not bear it.

And then he saw her.

A very unwise choice.

Sitting on the sofa, her laptop on her knee, her blonde hair high in a ponytail and with credit card in hand. He saw her blush as he entered, though she didn't look at him.

He didn't have to even be there to make her blush this morning.

Just her thought process last night made her burn with shame.

He could have taken her on the balcony, had he chosen to. He could have come to her room and taken her then—what sort of babysitter was she? She wanted to get away from the palace today, wanted to clear her mind before it went back to thinking of him. She'd expected his talk with his father to take for ever, that by the time they were finished she'd be long gone, but instead he walked up behind her.

'What are you doing?' he asked as she tapped on her computer. Most people wouldn't look, Georgie thought. Most people wouldn't come up behind you and stare over your shoulder at the page you were on, and even if they did, most people would pretend not to be taking an interest.

Ibrahim, though, wasn't like most people. Georgie was scared to turn, her skin prickling at his closeness, the air between them crackling with energy.

'I'm booking a tour.'

'A tour?'

'Of the desert.'

'Scroll down.'

She really couldn't believe his audacity.

'Are you always this…?' She couldn't even sum it up in one word—rude, nosy? And then when clearly she hadn't followed his command quickly enough, when clearly she hadn't jumped to his bidding in time, he leant over her shoulder, moved her hand to the side and scrolled down for himself. In that second Georgie found her word—invasive.

'An authentic desert experience…' Every word was mocking. 'You are staying at the palace, your sister is a princess and you are considering a guided tour?'

'Felicity is busy,' Georgie sighed.

'With Jamal?'

'No. Karim is heading out to the west today to assess

the situation with the Bedouins—he wanted her to go with him, and she agreed. She won't be back till late.'

'So why aren't you auditioning for the part of nanny? Didn't she ask you to watch Azizah today?'

'She did.' Georgie gave a guilty blush. 'But I said no. I said that I'd seen she was busy and had already made plans for the next couple of days.'

'Bad Aunty.'

'Good Aunty,' Georgie said, because she had given this a lot of thought when feeding Azizah overnight. 'I want to be her aunt, not her nanny. So when Felicity asked this morning if I could watch her, I told her I had plans.' She rolled her eyes. 'Now I just have to make them.'

'You can't go on a tour.' He shook his head. 'That is like asking me to dinner and then I have to ring for a take-away.'

He was angry after his talk with his father; restless and confined, and in a moment his mind was made up. 'I will take you.'

'I don't think that's the best idea.' Georgie swallowed, imagining Felicity's reaction.

'It's a very good idea.' Ibrahim said, because two days in, his homesickness had gone. Two days in Zaraq and he remembered why he'd left in the first place. 'You should see the desert—and I would like to go there too.' He would face his demons head on. The desert did not call him—the desert was not a person or a thing. Yes, maybe he had taken his horse only to the edge this visit or had ridden it on the beach, but he would go to the

desert today because he refused to fear it. He would give
Georgie her day and then he would leave. 'I'll tell them
to prepare the horses.'

'I had one riding lesson nearly a decade ago.' Georgie
said. 'I'll stick with my air-conditioned bus.'

'Then I'll drive you.'

Insane, probably.

'Look, I don't think my sister would approve and it
has nothing to do with…' Her voice trailed off. After
all, why shouldn't she go out with Ibrahim? Especially
with what he said next.

'You have to promise to keep your hands off me,
though.' He said it with a smile. 'Or our souls will be
bound for ever.' He rolled his eyes as he said it. 'It's a
load of rubbish, of course—I mean, look at my mother
and father. Still we'd better not take that chance.'

'I'm sure I can restrain myself.' Georgie smiled back.
'You're not that irresistible.'

'Liar.' He gave her a very nice smile. 'I'm saving you
for London.'

His presumption did not irritate, instead it warmed.
That she might see him again without all the confines
brought hope without compromise.

'Ring Felicity now, tell her you have booked a tour,'
Ibrahim said, 'with an experienced guide…'

Blushing even though she was on the phone, Georgie
did that, but instead of questions and a demand for details from Felicity all she got was guilty relief.

'What if she finds out?'

'How would she?'

'Won't the staff say something?'

'I'll smuggle you out,' Ibrahim said. 'I'll have them pack me lunch. They always pack enough for ten—they are used to me heading out.'

'Are you sure?'

He wasn't.

Not sure of anything, and least of all her.

A woman who changed her mind at less than a moment's notice, a woman his brother had warned him against yet again just this very morning, was serious trouble.

And there was unfinished business, which did not sit well with Ibrahim.

Still, where they were heading, there could be no conclusion, for the desert had rules of it own.

'I would like to spend the day with you.'

It was the only thing he knew.

CHAPTER EIGHT

HE FROWNED at her carefully planned desert wardrobe when she climbed into his Jeep.

Cool capri pants, a T-shirt and flat pumps were clearly not what he had been expecting her to change into.

'See if your sister has robes.'

'I'm not wearing them!' Georgie said. 'Anyway, on the tour guidelines it said—'

'That was for a play date. This is the real thing,' Ibrahim interrupted. 'You'll get burnt.'

'I've got sunblock on.'

'Don't come crying to me then at 3 a.m.,' Ibrahim said, and then he changed his mind, gave her a flash of that dangerous smile. 'Well, you are welcome to— just don't expect sympathy.' And Georgie swallowed, because they *were* flirting and a day in the desert, a whole day alone with him, was something she hadn't dared dream of and certainly not with him looking like *that*.

He *was* dressed for the desert and it was an Ibrahim she had not once glimpsed or envisaged. The sight made her toes curl in her unsuitable pumps, for if her mind could have conjured it up, this was how she'd have envisioned him. A man of the desert in white robes, his feet encased in leather straps and a black and white kafeya that hid his hair from sight and allowed more focus on his face.

'What?' Ibrahim asked, as he often did to silence.

'Bring it back,' Georgie said, and they were definitely flirting because he smiled as he registered what she meant.

'Consider it packed.'

They drove for miles, until the road ran out. Then Ibrahim hurtled the Jeep over the dunes, accelerating and braking, riding the dunes like a surfer on a wave. He had been wrong to fear it, Ibrahim decided, because all it was was fairy-tales and sand.

He parked near a vast canyon, with a few clusters of shrubs and not much else.

'Is this it?' Georgie asked, curious at her own disappointment.

'This is it,' Ibrahim said. 'You take the rug and I'll bring the food over.'

'Where?'

'To the picnic table,' he teased.

'Ha, ha,' she said as she stepped out. She knew she was being a bit precious, or just plain shallow—she didn't want belly dancers or for Ibrahim to produce a hookah. She'd just dreamt of it so, built it up to something majestic in her mind, and all there was…was nothing. She felt the blistering heat on her head and she scanned the horizon, trying to get her bearings, to see the city and the palace behind, or the blue of the ocean that circled the island, but there was nothing but endless sand.

'What direction is the palace?'

'That way,' Ibrahim said, spreading a blanket at the side of the Jeep for shade. She sat down and accepted some iced mint and lemon tea, but her eyes could not accept the nothingness.

'You want camels?' He grinned.

'I guess,' she admitted. 'And I'd love to see the desert people.'

'We might come across some. But most are deeper in the desert.'

'What is this illness that the Bedouins are suffering from?' Georgie asked.

'A virus,' Ibrahim explained. 'It is not serious with treatment, and most have been vaccinated. Most in Zaraqua anyway, but out of the city…' He looked out to the horizon. 'Beyond the royal tent there is nothing to the west. It is accessible only by helicopter. There is no refuelling point, no roads…'

'What if they need help?'

'It is how they choose to live.' Ibrahim repeated his father's words, though today they did not sit well in his gut. 'Ten years ago there was talk, contractors were bought in, proposals made, but the elders protested they did not want change and so, instead we concentrated on the town, the hospital and university.'

He watched her wriggle on the blanket, her capri pants and linen shirt uncomfortable now and her cheeks pink. Instead of saying 'I told you so', he headed to the vehicle and retrieved a scarf, which he tied for her, and it was bliss to have relief.

'Here.' As he sat down he pulled something from the sand and he handed her a shell. 'You are protected—that is what they mean.'

'There really are shells? From when it was ocean?'

'Maybe,' Ibrahim said. 'Or maybe a small animal. There are more questions than answers.' He smeared some thick white cheese on bread and offered it to her, but Georgie took a sniff and shook her head.

'I don't like goat's cheese.'

'Neither do I,' Ibrahim said, 'when it is from a high-street store. Try it.' He held it to her mouth and it was a gesture Georgie usually could not tolerate. Despite her healing, still there were boundaries and unwittingly he had crossed one. He held the morsel to her lips, told her what she should eat, only his black eyes caressed her as they did so, and there was, for the first time in this situation, the absence of fear. 'Try,' he teased, 'and my apologies if it is not to your taste.'

It was to her taste; there was a note to it that she could not detect and he watched as those blue eyes tried to work it out.

'The goats graze only on thyme,' Ibrahim explained. 'It makes this a rare delicacy.'

And she tasted other things.

Fruits she had never heard of that had been dried by the desert sun. She felt cool beneath the scarf. She felt brave in his company and not scared of the silence when they lay back on the rug for a while—and she knew he would not kiss her, knew, despite the energy that thrummed between them, that their day must end soon. They had driven for hours and there was only half a tank of fuel, but she wanted something else from the desert.

She wanted more.

'You would get a greater sense of it if I left you alone.' He spoke to her as he looked at the sky.

She smiled at him. 'I'd be bored out of my skull.'

'No,' Ibrahim said. 'That is how they make you fear it.' His face turned to hers and they lay on the rug, just talking, sure that they would play by the rules. 'When I was four or five, my father brought me. I was the same as you. Bored with the picnic...'

'I'm not bored.' Georgie corrected. 'I'm not bored with you.'

'Bored,' he said. 'That was how I felt, and unimpressed really, and then my father climbed into the Jeep and his aide drove off. I thought they had forgotten me, that it was a mistake, but, no, it was done to all of us.'

'They left you here.' She was appalled.

'They watch you apparently from a distance, but you don't know that. It is to make you strong. When it is just you, when you are alone, then you are in awe of it.'

'And did it make you strong?'

'No.' Ibrahim grinned. 'I cried and I sat down and I cried some more, I cried till I vomited and then I cried some more when my father whipped me for being weak, which I was.' He shrugged. He told the truth because he would never let them shame him for how he had felt, and that was what had angered his father most. 'I wanted my mother.'

'That's so cruel.' Georgie couldn't believe it. 'That won't happen to Azizah.'

'No.'

'What if they have a son?'

'Could you imagine Felicity?' He laughed at that thought and so too did Georgie. 'I think we can safely say any future nephew will be spared that particular induction. Do you want me to drive off now?' he asked. 'To leave you alone with it for a while?'

'No,' Georgie said, because the thought made her shiver, but she did still want more from the desert. 'Can we wait for the sunset?'

He turned his face skywards.

'Sunset is hours away.'

'Can we stay?'

And, no, they could not sit in the desert for hours—he could, for he had done his time in the land, but she was fair underneath the scarf and not used to the heat. He was about to tell her so but then something more fleeting than a thought changed his mind.

'We can go to the tent,' he offered. 'We can wait there for sunset. There are horses we can ride if you wish. I will find you a docile one. I can refuel. Bedra, the housekeeper, will be there with her husband. It is a royal tent, it is ready always for the princes or the king.' And he sounded very confident, as if he were suggesting they stop off at a café for coffee on the way home. Yet he had not been back to the tent in years and it was not a prospect he usually relished—but for reasons unknown even to himself he wanted to show her.

'What if Felicity—?'

'Why do you need her permission?' Ibrahim asked, a bit irritated now, but not at her, more at himself for his stupid offer. He had no desire to go to the tent and was rather hoping she would refuse. 'You are your own person. Do you want to come or not?'

'Please.'

She did not really understand the change in him, for he whipped up the blanket and threw it in the vehicle, threw the remains of their food for the unseen wildlife and Georgie took off her scarf. They drove in tense silence and maybe it was because of too much sun because she certainly wasn't relaxed in his company now. Still, she must have nodded off because she woke up with her head against the window to find his mood not improved by his unresponsive passenger or the increasing winds that threw sand against the windscreen and screamed around the vehicle. Inside the car it was almost dark, the sky bathed in browns and gold, and he had the sat-nav on. Ibrahim glanced over briefly as she stirred beside him.

'We're in a sandstorm?'

'We have been for the last hour,' Ibrahim said. 'We will just refuel and then leave. You wouldn't be able to see the sunset anyway. I will have Bedra prepare us some refreshments and then we will head back to the palace.'

'Isn't it dangerous?'

'If you don't know what you are doing,' Ibrahim said. 'We'll be fine.' Even though he sounded confident, he wasn't so sure. Visibility was extremely low and worsening and could change to zero in a matter of seconds. Really, unless the storm passed they would have to wait it out at the tent. He had even considered halting the Jeep but if the storm worsened they could find themselves buried, so he had decided to head for the tent and assess things then.

Ibrahim had listened to the warnings before they'd left, would never have brought her out here had he known a storm was building, but even listening to the radio now, tuning in for updates, still there was no mention of this storm. He glanced as her hand fiddled with an air vent. 'Leave it closed,' Ibrahim barked, and then checked himself. She really had no idea just how dangerous this was.

'Why have we stopped?'

'Because we are here.'

They were. Beyond the curtain of sand Georgie could just make out material billowing a few metres away.

'Wait there,' Ibrahim said. 'I will come and get you.'

She didn't need him to open her door and ignoring him Georgie climbed out herself and immediately realised Ibrahim hadn't been being chivalrous. The sand tore at her hands as she moved to cover her eyes, the scream of the wind shrilled in her ears, filled her mouth and nose and in a moment, in less than a moment, she was lost, completely and utterly lost. The vehicle was surely just a step or two behind her, the tent somewhere in front, but it was like being spun around in blind man's buff. Completely disorientated, she felt something akin to panic as she glimpsed for the very first time the might of the desert, and then she felt a wedge of muscle, felt Ibrahim's thick white robe and his arm pulling her, smothering her face and eyes with his kafeya. He guided her from the screaming wind, every step an effort, until she felt the wall of the tent in front of her and then the bliss of relative peace as he pushed her inside.

The peace didn't last long.

She coughed out sand. He lit an oil lamp and his expression was less than impressed when it came into view in the flare of the flame. Her coughing died down.

'When I tell you to wait—you wait.'

'I was trying to…' To what? Her voice trailed off. To show him she didn't need her door opened? To show her independence in the middle of a storm? There wasn't a single appropriate response.

'I'm not sure if you're naïve or ignorant.' Ibrahim was furious. 'You could have died.' He showed no mercy and neither did he exaggerate. 'In the time it took me to get around that vehicle, you could have been lost. *Listen to me!*' he roared. 'In a storm, and one as severe as this one is becoming, you can be lost in a moment—or choked by the sand. It is that simple.'

'I'm sorry…' she said, but Ibrahim wasn't listening.

'Bedra!' He shouted. 'Where is everyone?'

He strode into the darkness, lighting lamps as he

went, revealing more and more beauty with each flare of light. The floor a scatter of rugs, the tent walls hung with them too, and there were ornaments, instruments she didn't recognise. It was the desert she'd dreamt of and she wandered in quiet appreciation as Ibrahim grew more irate, walking down white corridors that led to separate areas. He called down them all.

'There's a note.' Georgie found it as Ibrahim searched for the staff. 'At least, I think it's a note.'

She handed it to him and watched his expression turn to one of incredulity as he read it. 'Why would Bedra and her husband be out helping with the sick? Their job is to tend to the desert palace—they should be here at all times.'

'Well, given that she is a doctor, maybe her skills were better needed elsewhere,' Georgie responded, and then instantly regretted it, because from the frown on his proud features she realized, he didn't know. Felicity had told her about the secret desert work that she and Karim did for the Bedouins, the mobile clinic they ran, how Bedra was so much more than a maid. She had assumed that even if the king didn't know, Ibrahim would—he was Karim's brother after all—but clearly he hadn't been told.

'She's not a doctor,' Ibrahim said derisively. 'She's a housekeeper. She should be here.'

But as they explored the empty tent, clearly there were things that Ibrahim did not know, because beyond the servants' quarters, where royals would never venture, was a treatment area as well stocked as any modern doctor's surgery.

'I'm not sure,' Georgie could not resist as Ibrahim surveyed it, 'if you're naïve or just ignorant.'

She wondered if she had pushed him too far, but he conceded with a slight shrug and a shake of the head. 'Clearly I'm ignorant,' he said. 'She's really a doctor?'

'I shouldn't have said anything. I hope I haven't got Karim into trouble.'

'As if I'm going to tell on him. So that's why he was always out in the desert? I was wondering what his problem was—how much contemplation one man needed?'

He did make her laugh, but it changed into a cough and Ibrahim was still cross with himself for placing her in danger. 'I checked before we came out...there was no indication of a storm as big as this one. It seems to have come from nowhere.'

'Are there lots of them?'

Ibrahim nodded. 'But this is severe.'

'Could the tent blow away?'

Ibrahim just laughed. 'They are designed for these conditions.' And then he went into engineer mode, talking about vents and rigging, but Georgie had other things on her mind.

'Will Felicity and Karim be all right?' She thought of them out there and her heart started racing.

'They will be fine,' he assured her. 'Karim will know exactly what to do. They will be waiting it out like us. They just won't be able to fly back.'

'Felicity will be frantic.' Georgie closed her eyes. 'I should have stayed at the palace and looked after Azizah.'

'In case her mother got caught in a storm?' Ibrahim shook his head. 'You can't think like that.' The wind screeched a warning and Ibrahim knew when he was beaten. 'We will stay till it passes, but I think we are here for the night.' They headed back out to the lounge area and he stood as she roamed, watched her expression as she looked at the wall hangings and her nosy little fingers picked up priceless heirlooms and weighed them. He would never have planned this. Would never have bought her here if he'd know they would be alone.

Her cheeks were pink from the sun and her arms just a little bit sunburnt. Her clothes were grubby and her hair wild from the sand and the wind. And how he wanted her. Though he would not blatantly defy the desert, he would follow the rules while he was here, but his way.

Ibrahim did not have to chase, all he had was the thrill of the catch. He had never had to want or wait or been said no to—except once.

And here she was.

With him tonight, and now he didn't want to wait till London.

Tonight he would sample the thrill of the chase; tonight he would make certain that she would not refuse him again. He would romance her, feed her, turn on every ounce of his undeniable charm—he would ripen her with his mind and let her simmer overnight. They would rise early, Ibrahim decided, she could see the sunrise and then he would take her to a hotel and bed her, take her ripe and ready and plump and delicious. And he wouldn't even need to reach out. She would fall into his hands without plucking.

In fact, he decided with a smile, she would beg.

'What?' Georgie asked, seeing a smile pass over his face.

'I was just thinking. You will have your authentic desert experience. Bedra will have left food, the table is set, we can feast tonight, and tomorrow, and when the storm is past you can rise early and see the sunrise.' He saw a flicker of a frown on her face, but he moved to relax her. 'We must have separate rooms. Come, I'll show you the guest quarters.'

They walked through the lounge, the air thick and warm, and she glimpsed a large curtained area with a bed so high and deep you would almost need stairs and a springboard to dive into it. The room was heavy with scent—musky, exotic oils that aroused, to ensure future generations, and the bed throbbed with colour, drapes and cushions. He let her eyes linger for more than a moment, made sure she had seen it, and then gently he took her elbow.

'That is mine. Your room is over here.'

It was thirty-four steps away, she knew because she counted the distance between their rooms. Ibrahim knew she would be counting them again in her head later, for though hers was absolutely beautiful, for royal guest,

not a princess, and just that tiny bat of her eyelashes
told him she knew.

'It's lovely,' Georgie said, because it was.

It was!

Apart from the palace, it was absolutely the nicest
room she had ever been a guest in, and she told herself
that again as she enthused and thanked him, but her
mind was somehow in his room, with heavy silk spreads
and a bed you could drown in. 'Here.' Ibrahim was supremely polite. 'Make use of the guest quarters as you
please.' He pulled back a drape and the space pulsed
with colour and rich fabrics.

'I can't just wear someone's things.'

'These are for guests who arrive unprepared.' He
slowly looked around the room. 'Nothing changes...'
There was a pensive note to his voice, but he didn't
elaborate. 'I will leave you to bathe, just help yourself
to anything. Perhaps dress for dinner?'

'Dress?'

'You wanted an authentic desert experience, well, let
me give you one.' He watched her swallow. 'I'll prepare
the lounge.'

Despite the ancient ornaments and artefacts, there
was every modern convenience and Georgie filled the
heavy bath with steaming water and chose from the
array of fragrant oils. After several hours in the Jeep
and the grit and the sand she had accumulated, it was
bliss to stretch out in the warm, scented water. She could
have lain for ages, except she really was hungry.

Georgie had had no intention of selecting clothing from the guests' wardrobe.

A charity cupboard stocked for inappropriate guests she did not need, and she wasn't keen on the idea of playing dress up. Except maybe she was, because she thought of Ibrahim in his robes in London and there were still angry red marks on her waist where her capri pants had cut into her, and the pale fabric that had looked so cool and elegant on the hanger in the high-street store was now crumpled and rather grubby.

Georgie flicked through the wardrobe: vast kaftans that would swamp her delicate frame. And what was it with Zaqar and shades of yellow? Yet her first brisk hand movements grew slower, her eyes drawn to the intricate beading and embroidery, every piece a work of art. They were in decreasing sizes too, she realised, for there near the end was a slim robe in a dark blood red with small glass beads on the front and a dance of gold leaves around the hem—it was nothing like something she would ever choose for herself, but was perhaps the most beautiful article of clothing she had ever seen.

The fabric slid coolly beneath her fingers, the finest of silks. It beckoned, and she closed her eyes in bliss as she gave in and slid it over her head. It skimmed her body. As she looked in the mirror and saw a different Georgie, her stomach tightened in strange recognition at the woman who met her gaze. Not a girl or a young woman but a woman with all awkwardness gone, and it bewildered her. It was as if the fragrant bath had surgically removed that awkwardness, because she liked what she saw and wanted to enhance it. Her eyes glanced down to the heavy brushes and flat glass containers filled with rich colours to perfume bottles, and she pulled the stopper from one and inhaled the musky scent, she wanted to dress for him. She wanted her night in the desert.

Ibrahim's catering skills ran to ringing his favourite restaurant and telling them the number of guests. His kitchen in London was stocked and maintained by his housekeeper. At the palace, occasionally at night he wandered in and chatted to the overnight chef, who would prepare Ibrahim a late-night or rather pre-dawn snack, but here in the desert things were different—here, a young prince was left for a period to fend for himself. Not that he had to this evening, for Bedra *was* both a doctor and royal housekeeper. When he opened the third fridge, there were platters fit for a king, or should a reprobate prince happen by, and there were jugs too, all lined up and ready, that had herbs measured and prepared. All Ibrahim had to do was add water and carry trays through, but he was pleased with his handiwork. He even lit some candles and incense and turned on some music to soften the noise of the wind. Then he headed to his quarters to bath and change.

Ibrahim shaved, which he did not normally do in the desert, but his face was rough and as watched the blade slice over his chin, he thought of Georgie's cheeks, of her mouth and her face and, yes, deny it as he may, he was preparing himself for her.

Preparing himself for tomorrow, Ibrahim warned himself, because this tent was a place you brought your bride. This was a place where the union was sealed and even if he didn't strictly believe in the tradition, tonight he would respect it.

He headed out to the lounge area. He wanted to eat and wondered what was taking her so long, because he was ready and had *prepared* dinner too. But every moment of waiting was worth it as, looking just a little bit shy but definitely not awkward, she came to him.

'You look…' He did not finish, he could not finish, because not only did she look beautiful as she stood with her long blonde hair coiling as it dried, her skin flushed from the warm water, somehow she looked as if she came from the desert. Somehow, despite her pale features, despite it all, she looked as if she belonged here, and Ibrahim wondered if this night, together but apart, was more than he should have taken on.

Wondered how far he should tease her.

Her eyes were very blue in her pale face. She had none of that kohl that sharpened them, just a shimmer of silver on her lids that glittered each time she blinked. It was her mouth that had been painted, in the same blood red as her dress, and it trembled a little as his eyes fell on it, and it killed him that he must wait till tomorrow to kiss it.

She sat on the floor at the low table and Ibrahim did the same. He had seen her a little nervous around food, but now her eyes were just curious. The nerves, he knew, were for another reason, for long before she had sat down he had seen the leaping pulse in her throat, the glitter not just on her eyelids but in eyes that shone with arousal.

'Here.' He handed her a heavy fruit, which looked like a cross between a peach and an apple, and selected one for himself. As she went to take a tentative bite he shook his head. 'It is marula, you drink it.' He squeezed the heavy fruit between his fingers and she watched as sticky goo ran between them. He selected a straw and plunged it into the fruit and he took her mind to mad places, because the fruit was her flesh and she held her breath as he pierced it.

'You,' he said, and she broke the skin of her fruit, not as easily as him but it worked and she drank from it. Though the fluid was sweet and warm and delicious, somehow she wanted to lean and lick the moisture still damp on his fingers.

She ate, and it was different, because she was thinking about food again, about every morsel that slid down her throat, but it was far from with loathing, because each swallow of her throat was watched by him—and she wanted his mouth there.

She wanted their tongues to meet in one half of the pomegranate, but he offered her only her share and then ate his.

'No spoons.' Ibrahim said, and made eating seem debauched, but in the most thrilling of ways, and for the first time there was regret that a meal was over. As they moved to the couches, she wanted back at his table.

And Ibrahim knew.

But it was safer on the sofa and she sipped sweet coffee gratefully and had another cup to help her sober up, because that was how he sometimes made her feel.

'The trouble with antiques,' Ibrahim drawled, filling her cup with the jug that had been used since his childhood, 'is that nothing gets thrown out. Nothing changes. Always it is the same.'

'You hate it here?'

'No.' Ibrahim said, and then went on, 'Not always.' He saw her confusion. 'I know every corner of this tent. We came as children—it was good then.' He didn't want to talk, he wanted to slowly seduce, he wanted her wanting him in the morning, but somehow she demanded, without him always realising, more from him.

Sometimes he found himself talking with her, not about things that teased but things that tortured. He heard his voice saying things he had never said before, and she didn't just listen, as others would have, she did not agree but partook.

'When your mother was here? Was it after she left when it changed?' she probed, and he closed his eyes, but her question remained and he thought about it, because when his mother had been here, it had been different. Then his father would laugh and the children would play and spend a whole day searching for one rare wild flower for the maid to put on their mother's breakfast tray. He and Ahmed would play in a cave a morning's walk from here and the servants would find them at dusk, but the scolding had always been worth it.

Then there had been no fear when he had been with Ahmed, just the arrogance of youth, for surely nothing could harm the young princes.

'It just changed,' Ibrahim said.

'After Ahmed died?'

She had gone where no one should, where not even he dared.

'For him I would have been king.' He was beyond angry, his voice was raw. 'Had he just asked me, had he even bothered to tell me his fears. Instead…' He could not forgive his brother, and that killed a part of Ibrahim too, and he could not linger on it either, so he spoke of other things instead. 'It changed for many reasons. For a while it was a playground, but at seventeen you spend a month alone before you go to the military. It is a time of transition. For a month you wander and then return to the tent.'

'No staff?'

'None,' Ibrahim said. 'You remember the fear when you were left as a child, but there is no one watching this time. So slowly you build up for the walk home.'

'You walk home?' She could not keep the shock from her voice—that a teenager would be left to fend for himself then walk for miles. 'And then you get to join the army—some reward!'

'No.' Ibrahim shook his head. 'First you become a man. There is a very good reason to find your bearings and keep walking back to the palace. There, waiting, is your reward.'

Georgie blinked and as his eyes never left her face, as realisation slowly dawned, her pale skin darkened. 'That's disgusting,' Georgie spluttered.

'Why?' He was genuinely bemused. 'I am a royal prince—the woman I marry must be a virgin. It is my duty to be a skilled lover.'

'To teach her!' Georgie spat.

'Of course.' Ibrahim said. 'But even a teacher first has to be taught.'

'You make it sound so clinical.'

'When?' He challenged. 'You interpret it as clinical—I assure you it was not.'

'You can't *teach* it…' she flared but right there her argument started to weaken, because in his arms she had learnt so much. 'It isn't just…' she tried again, but words failed her. 'Some things,' she attempted, and then closed her eyes in defeat, because how could she admit that it wasn't just his skill that brought her to frenzy, it was him.

That just the curve of his arrogant mouth and the scent of his skin prompted vigilance, that if he sat there now and did not move, if all he did was stay still as she leant over and kissed him, if all he did was lie there as her hands roamed his body, it would be every bit as good as her recall. It wasn't Ibrahim's skill her body craved— it was him. 'When we…' Georgie swallowed. There was something she needed to say. 'When I stopped you, it wasn't because—'

'I don't want to discuss it,' Ibrahim said, because it would be too dangerous here to recall that night. Going into the details of their time together would not help.

'Please. I want—'

'You heard what I said.'

He could be so rude. Annoyed at him, angry at how he just closed off whenever it suited him. She refused to drag conversation out of him. She wandered around the lounge and there was much to amuse and interest her. She ran her fingers along one instrument and another and for the first time in her life she actually wanted to dance. She wanted to turn up the music and turn to him, and she felt as if she was fighting insanity, wondered just what it was in the fruit, because the desert made her dizzy with freedom from inhibition. She forced herself to explore rather than linger, picked up a heavy glass bottle and pulled out the stopper, but Ibrahim came over.

'They are not for cosmetic...' Ibrahim shook his head, took the glass jar and replaced the stopper. 'They are medicinal.'

'I know,' Georgie answered, irritated. 'This is what I study.'

'These are potent.'

'I do know!' She saw the dismissal in his single blink. It was a reaction she was used to, yet from Ibrahim it annoyed her. 'Just because you don't believe in my work...'

'But I do.'

'So why are you so scorning?'

'I am not...' His voice trailed off, because in truth he was. 'There are thousands of years of learning, of wisdom in these oils, our ways—'

'That can't be learnt in a four-week course!' Stupidly she felt like crying, not at his scorn, not at his derision, but because she felt there was truth in what he was saying. It was a question she had asked herself. She had sat in a classroom and later with clients wondering if she was worthy of imparting such ancient knowledge.

'Do you believe in what you do?' Ibrahim asked.

'Of course,' Georgie said. 'Well, I do, but I know there is more, much more to learn.'

'Always there is more to learn, for ever there will be more to learn,' Ibrahim said.

'So you don't think I should practise.'

'I did not say that. I go for my massage in London. There are practitioners like you...' He said it without scorn. 'They work with the oils, but their minds are not present.' How could he explain something he did not fully understand himself? But Georgie understood.

'Mine is,' she said, and took the bottle back from him. She held it a moment then took off the stopper, placed a drop of oil on her finger and moved it to his throat. He stood rigid as her finger slid down to his throat and in tiny circular motions massaged over his thymus—that area held past issues and his was full. She could smell the frankincense, the bergamot and a note she couldn't identify, and still her finger circled and her mind was present. It was Ibrahim who pulled back.

'This is what you do for a living?' He captured her hand.

'You make it sound like I'm running some seedy massage parlour. It's about energy and healing and relaxation.' She gave an impatient shake of her head. 'I don't have to explain to you what I do.'

He dropped his grip and still her finger circled. 'Show me,' Ibrahim said, which normally would have been a dangerous tease, an extension of his game, but it was more than that. He could feel the tiny flickers of her pulse in the pads of her fingers, and he also wanted some of this peace she talked about. 'Show me,' he said again.

He was used to massage—a keen horseman, there was all too often a hip or a shoulder that had taken a beating. He used massage just for physical ailments but wanted more. Often in London he found himself face down on a table, but no matter how skilled the hands, no matter how they relaxed his body, his mind did not quieten, and it was that he craved—some peace and clarity, for conflicting thoughts to still so he could assess them. For a second she had given him that quietness and he wanted more.

He pulled off his robes and lay on the cushioned floor. Just a sash covered him and it was Georgie who was awkward as she prepared her oils from the vast selection. It was she who was facing the biggest test, she wondering how to remain professional because he was utterly and completely exquisite. She was used to shy, fragile women, and there could be no greater contrast.

His back gleamed with muscle and awaited her touch, but there was a pertinent problem and as she prepared her dishes and vials she tried to keep her voice matter-of-fact.

'You need to lie on your back.'

She watched his shoulders stiffen, watched his expanded chest still as he held air in, then he turned round and she covered him, because this was not about sex, this was about something more.

But for Ibrahim any hope of relaxing, of merely enjoying a feminine touch, was dashed then, because lying like this with her kneeling next to him, it would take every ounce of concentration he possessed to ignore her, not to give in to the natural response of his body. He must lie there now and think of things, anything other than the woman who was moving down to his feet. He must not think of the hands she rubbed together to warm in preparation and he was about to roll over, to tell her not to bother, but as she captured a foot her fingers were so silky and oiled he lingered.

She had felt him resist, felt him fight, but as her hands slid to his feet and she stroked his sole, there was a tentative surrender that she recognised, a shift when a mind handed itself over to you. She wasn't sure if that trust was merited. Just a ping of doubt went through her as she thought of a four-week course versus the arts of the desert, then she knew what to do, and there was no more trepidation. She felt as if the roof had lifted from the tent, felt as if it was daylight again and the wind was gone, that the sun was beating directly into her head, spreading through her body and warming her fingers. Her hands knew what to do, and Georgie gave in to the healing along with Ibrahim and did what the desert told her.

She oiled his feet with lavender and spruce, worked slowly up past his calves, and when his legs were oiled and his body relaxed, her mind with his, she oiled her fingers and moved to his navel. There was a brief hesitation as her fingers hovered, and then it was only about him and she worked gently there with jasmine and neroli. She moved to his chest, small clockwise motions around his heart, and she couldn't hear the wind, just its message, and she worked on forgiveness with geranium and other drops of different oils, but she still felt resistance, his urge for her to move on. She moved to his stomach again. She worked on release, with ylang ylang and blue tansy, but he would not give in to it.

She added melissa, the fragrance he had smelt on her that night on the balcony, or as he called it—Bal-smin. It was the chief of oils and Ibrahim met his match in it. She saw his eyes close tighter, and if it had not been Ibrahim, so proud and removed, she would have sworn it was a man fighting back tears. Then she felt the release, felt the pain slide out beneath her fingers as he freed Ahmed. And then she went to his heart again, which didn't need her hand now because he had forgiven, and her hand slid down his body, down his legs, then to his feet to finish.

And it was more than intimate, it was more than sex, it was the closest he had ever been to another person, and when she had finished, when he opened his eyes, he willed her to go on. But she could hear the music and see the man before her now, and it wasn't her vocation that led her—it was instinct. She watched her own fingers as they dripped oil low on his stomach, and it was the woman she had only today first seen in the mirror that peeled back the sash. Her warm hands slipped around him, stroked him while she looked at him, slid both palms around in a skilled motion she had never so much as attempted before, and he looked into eyes that were wanton and a red mouth that in moment would take him—and how he wanted it to.

'We cannot be together here.'

She could feel him sliding through her fingers, could feel the beat of her heart in her throat, and it was him and only him that made her bold.

'No one would have to know.' He watched her lips part in a smile. 'What happens in the desert stays in the desert.'

Ibrahim's fingers moved up her chin and slid into her hair and how he wanted to guide her head down, rather than wait till the morning. He wanted to break a rule, but he was stronger than that, or was he weak, because he could not defy the desert.

'This is how you work?'

He watched colour flood her face, ached unfulfilled as her hands released him.

'Of course not.'

'Go to bed.' he stood and pulled her from her knees to her feet and felt guilty for shaming her. He fought a rare need to explain himself, that it was safer if they were apart. 'Anyway, you might change your mind again at the last minute. Just go to bed, Georgie.'

CHAPTER NINE

It was the longest night and she lay there both embarrassed and wanting.

The air was thick and warm and soon her jug of water was empty. Georgie wanted to go to the kitchen to replenish it, but was scared to move.

She had tried to seduce him. She closed her eyes in mortification—with all her banging on about being professional, she could hardly believe what she'd done, what the desert had made her do.

Georgie. She could hear him calling her.

Georgie. She heard it again and stood.

Georgie. It was his voice, she was sure of it, and she padded across the room, parting the drape, ready for his summons, but then she heard the shriek of laughter from the wind that taunted her and she ran back to bed and curled up, wondering if she was going mad.

Ibrahim. He heard it too, but he was prepared for it. He heard the desert tease, heard the wind drop into a low seductive voice that danced around his bed, saw her face in his dream and when he awoke, when he could not sleep, when his teeth gritted and his head thrashed with insomnia, his hand stalled on its way down to private solace, for even that release was denied him by the laws that bound him tonight, because he would have been thinking of her.

And sunrise should have brought relief, but there was none. Still the winds blacked it out as they screamed, still it was dark, and she heard his chant of prayer and finally she completely agreed with Ibrahim, for Georgie now hated the desert.

'Can we go?' she asked, when his prayers were completed and she padded out of her room.

'The winds are still heavy,' Ibrahim said but he did not look at her. 'Get dressed and we will have breakfast.'

'I'm not hungry.'

'Then go back to bed and rest,' he ordered. 'I will do the same. As soon as it is safe to do so, we will leave.'

'I'm scared,' Georgie admitted 'I'm scared of the noises…'

'It's just wind.'

'I feel like…' It sounded madder in words than in her head. 'I feel like it knows I mocked it last night.'

'Don't.' He loathed what he had said to her in an urgent attempt to halt what they had been doing. 'You did nothing wrong. I should not have spoken to you like that. Georgie…it's just tales I was telling.'

'You believe them.'

'No.' He shook his head. 'Yes. I don't know.' He didn't know. He could see her outline in the lamplight, he could hear the fear in her voice, and tales of old were illogical.

'Come here.'

She stood, scared to do as he said, scared to return to her own bed.

'Come on.'

His voice was real, the wind was not, and as the wind let out a screech, she ran those thirty-four steps to him, to the solid warmth of his arms. He could feel her heart hammering in her chest as he held her close, because she really was terrified.

'It's just…' He struggled for the words. 'Old wives' tales.'

'So they're not true?'

'No.' he started, but he could not quite deny them. 'I don't think so. Come…' His bed was warm and her skin was cold and he pulled her in.

'Did your parents not tell you tales when you were younger?'

'No.' She gave a cynical snort. 'We weren't exactly tucked in with a bedside story each night.'

'Is that why you ran away?' He felt her tense. 'Karim told me,' he admitted. 'Not everything, he was talking more about Felicity, about her childhood, how mistrusting it made her. Your father—'

'Was a drunken brute,' Georgie finished for him. 'My mother was terrified of him. Even after he died, he still left his mark on her. She's still taking tablets to calm her nerves, still scared of her own shadow.'

'What about you?'

'I wasn't scared of him—I just wanted to get away from him.'

'Which was why you ran?'

'I was always sent back.' She was angry at the memory, angry at the injustice. 'He never hit us—which made it fine, apparently. We were living in chaos, dancing to his temper, but…' She didn't want to talk about it, didn't want to relive those times again—times when the only thing she had been able to control had been the food that had gone into her mouth, but Ibrahim seemed to understand without her saying it. She felt his hand dust her arm and slip to her waist, to the slender frame that was softened now with slight curves. As her hands had helped him, his hands did their work now, each touch, each stroke assuring her somehow that he knew how hard fought each gain had been, how fiercely she had fought for survival.

He could not *not* kiss her.

Just a kiss, and as he moved to her mouth for a moment he fought it.

'What would happen?' Georgie whispered, and he could taste her sweet breath.

'Nothing probably.' With her next to him, he could rationalise it. 'As I said, look at my parents…'

'But they still love each other,' Georgie said. 'They're still bound. Felicity told me—' she did not know if she was betraying a secret '—that Karim wouldn't let her leave the desert till—'

'It's old wives' tales.' He was sure of it now. 'After

all, I can bring a mistress from the palace to the desert and I am not bound to her. It's just superstition.'

'Why doesn't she come to you?' Georgie asked. 'I mean, when you're younger. Why do you have to walk to the palace?' She liked the tales, liked hearing the stories.

'It would be different.' Ibrahim said. 'Your first time, at such a young age, you would not be able to separate the two—and if you love her in the desert…' It was too illogical to even try to explain it, so he smiled instead and felt her calm beside him. There was peace in his heart this morning that had been absent for ages, forgiveness in his soul, and he would be forever grateful to her for that, and he really could not not kiss her.

And that had caused trouble before, but this was a different kiss: this was slow and non-urgent and, a first for Ibrahim, it was a kiss that was purely tender.

And a kiss couldn't hurt when it felt so nice, and she was content with his kiss, because she'd craved it for months. The taste of his tongue and the weight of his lips. For a while Ibrahim too was content, to feel her breast through the fabric as his mouth explored hers, but then a kiss did not quite suffice, and he opened the buttons as far as they would go. 'Did your sister design this gown for you?' he teased, because even with all the buttons undone, he still couldn't get to her breast and his hand slid to her waist to pursue from a different angle, but that would not be wise so, just a little disgruntled, he pulled back.

His eyes asked permission, for what she didn't know,

but she licked her lips in consent and he tore the fabric and went back to kissing her. She felt his sigh of satisfaction in her mouth as his hand, unhindered now, met her breast, and she kissed him and felt the satin of his skin beneath her fingers. It was still just a kiss, though her hands roamed. They felt the chest she'd once touched and explored it again, felt the dark, flat nipple beneath the pads of her fingers. It remained at a kiss even as her hands slid down.

And then, recalling last night, there was hesitation, but his apology came by way of his hands that led her to him and he moaned in her mouth as she held him.

Still just a kiss as she touched and explored what all night she had thought of, then it was far more than a kiss because his mouth would not suffice and her lips trailed down his torso, tasting the salt of his skin till Ibrahim halted her, because he wanted more of her, wanted longer with her, than her mouth would allow.

'We mustn't.' Georgie said, as he pulled her body over his, because she was starting to understand there were rules.

'We won't,' Ibrahim said, because he had more control than anyone, that much he knew.

He liked living on the edge, the brink, and this morning he did just that. 'We can do this.' Ibrahim said, and he pulled her till her legs were astride him. He took a breast in his mouth and his hands slid over her bottom, and she steadied herself with her hands and thought she would die because it felt like heaven.

'We can't,' she said, which was different from the *I can't* she had once halted him with.

'We won't,' he insisted, as the tip of his thick length stroked her clitoris and he waited for the wind to warn him, or for a sign to halt him, or for Georgie to again recant. Except the desert was silent and there was nothing to halt him, and Georgie bit down on her lip to stop herself begging him to enter her.

She didn't need to.

He slipped in just a little way and she could never again say no to him, because he felt sublime.

And there was only one law that they followed, and that was nature's. He inched into her and then lifted her just a little further each time. He wanted the stupid nightdress off, but he did not want to stop touching her for a second. It was Georgie who lifted the fabric over her head and at the sight of her arms upstretched and her body above him he could no longer tease and cared nothing for rules, and he pulled her full down onto him.

The force of full entry had her cry in surprise, so purposefully and assuredly, he filled her, and though she tried to stretch for more of him, her body clamped down in possession, as if to assure herself she wouldn't flee from him again. He watched, he slid up on the cushions so he could watch them, and she saw more than passion in his eyes. She saw something else too and she wanted to share it, so he pushed her head down a little, so she could share in the dark and light they made. She loved the rules as she watched them unite, she wanted to be bound for ever. Then he guided her head to his and his cool tongue met hers—every beat of her orgasm matched his, every finger knotted in his hair met by the tug on her own scalp. Then, afterwards, their eyes were mirrors both searching for regret or dread at dues now to be paid, and both finding none.

She lay beside him, knew he was thinking and so too was she. 'Later today…' he kissed her shoulder, as if confirming a thought '…I will take you back to the palace and then I must leave for London.'

'You're leaving?'

'I have to go.'

She looked up at him.

'I need to speak properly with my father. I need to think about…' He didn't say 'us', but she was sure that he almost did. 'He has flown there today to visit my mother.'

'Because of what you said to him?'

'In spite of what I said to him.' The loathing in his voice did not match their tender mood.

'Is it always like this between you?'

'Always,' Ibrahim said. 'He demands I respect him—but how? Why can't he just let her go?'

'Let her go?' Georgie didn't understand. After all, his mother had her own life in London.

'She is still his wife.' Ibrahim looked down at her, took in the flushed cheeks and rumpled hair, and it felt so good to share his thoughts with her. 'She regrets her indiscretion—so much so that all this time she has stayed loyal.'

'But it's been years.'

'And there will be many more years. After all this time ignoring her, now he drops in at will. Who's to say next month, next year he will be too busy? And she is expected to wait.'

'Can't she divorce him?'

'There is no divorce in Zaraq. It is so forbidden that there is not even a word for it. A lacuna, there is no concept, no precedence. My mother knows that even if legally it is taken care of overseas, still always, to him, to the people of Zaraq, she is his wife and nothing can change it.'

He did not notice her flushed cheeks pale suddenly.

'There's nothing that can change it?'

'Nothing,' Ibrahim confirmed, and she felt her heart still. 'You cannot undo what is done—that is the rule of Zaraq.'

CHAPTER TEN

HAPPY its work had been done, the desert was silent and finally Ibrahim slept. Unlike on the plane, now, for the first time, he looked relaxed, and as she watched him, it was Georgie who was tense. She was starting to make sense of the strange rules, could see now what Felicity had been saying—that to the people of Zaraq she was still married.

Ibrahim would not mind, she tried to console herself. He would understand, she tried to convince herself, but wrapped in his arms she was unable to face him, felt like a liar, and she rolled over in shame.

At what point should she have said it?

Yesterday, or at the wedding? Was she supposed to walk up to someone and give them so much of herself on contact? But there had been opportunities, her conscience reminded her.

She had tried to tell him last night, but he had halted her, Georgie told herself, then guiltily admitted she had been relieved when he had stopped her, more than pleased to avoid seeing his face when she revealed the truth.

Georgie closed her eyes, and his arm wrapped around her, his warm, sleek body spooned in from behind. There was a possessiveness there that felt tender. There was a beauty in his embrace and a promise in his words that told her this had meant something to Ibrahim, that again they had glimpsed a future, but with what she knew now it was a future that again she might have to deny him. It was an uneasy sleep she fell into, filled with dreams of sacred oils and laughing winds, man-made structures and the sound of an engine.

'Get dressed.' His voice was urgent and jolted her awake. 'Someone is coming. I heard a helicopter.' The noise hadn't been a dream. She could hear the whir of the blades slowing. Surely there was time to race back to her room. All she had was a torn nightgown. He threw her a sash of cloth as he pulled on his clothes and she went to dash to her own quarters, but even as she stepped outside, she knew she had left it too late. She stood, shivering and embarrassed in the lounge area, and she couldn't look at Karim so she turned pleading eyes to Felicity, whose face was as white as chalk.

'Enjoying your tour?' Felicity sneered. 'So where's your *expert* guide?' Georgie was incredibly grateful when Ibrahim, dressed, thoroughly together and not remotely embarrassed, appeared from his chamber and took control.

'Your sister and I intended to return last night. There was a storm…'

'Enough!' Karim's shout was to silence his younger brother, but Ibrahim refused.

'Georgie, go and get dressed,' Ibrahim said, his voice supremely calm, 'and I will take you back to the palace.'

'Ibrahim,' Karim warned, but it fell on deaf ears.

'Go,' he said to Georgie. 'I will speak with my brother.' He eyed him darkly. 'We have done nothing wrong.'

'I warned you!' Karim shouted. 'I warned you to stay away from her.'

'And I chose not to listen. How dare you both walk in here with rage in your eyes and shame her? Have you forgotten how you met your wife?'

Georgie watched colour flood Felicity's cheeks— for their one night of passion had resulted in Azizah. But her sister seemed to have forgotten that fact as she followed Georgie to her room because Felicity was incensed. 'How could you, Georgie? This is my husband's family. You've been here a few days and you tumble into bed with him.'

'It wasn't like that.'

'Oh, please.'

'As Ibrahim said, you hardly waited before you jumped into bed with Karim,' Georgie retaliated.

'We weren't in Zaraq!' Felicity said. 'Here you play by the rules.'

'You know what?' Georgie had had enough. 'You really are starting to sound like them. What happened to my sister?'

'She grew up,' Felicity shouted. 'She behaved responsibly—but you were never very good at that were you, Georgie? Bunking off school, running away from home…' And Georgie could see the years of hurt she had caused in her sister's eyes, the hurt she had apologised for over and over again.

'I've done everything I can to help you and now you do this.' Felicity had tears streaming down her cheeks. 'I paid for your rehab when I couldn't afford it. Karim has helped too.'

'And I'm very grateful,' Georgie said, but she recalled Ibrahim's words and would not feel beholden.

'So this is how you show it!' Felicity shrilled.

Georgie did not break and she did not crumple, because all it was was a row, a confrontation that needed to be had, and no longer was she scared of it. 'I don't have to show anything.' Georgie said, her voice calm. 'I'm a different woman now; I'm a different person from who I was all those years ago. Ibrahim and I weren't just having a bit of fun.' She was sure of that, quite sure.

'It is fun to Ibrahim! Don't you get it? All this is to him is a diversion, a bit of fun to pass the time while he's here.'

'I don't have to prove him to you,' Georgie said.

I haven't got time for this.' Felicity shook her head. 'I have to wash and get changed and get back out there. They're loading the helicopter.'

'Can we just talk?' Georgie begged, because things needed to be said, the air needed to be cleared so they could both move on fully. 'Felicity please, I really need—'

'You always *need* something from me, Georgie, yet

you give nothing back.' Felicity shouted. 'Right now, I don't have time for it. There are people who are sick, you selfish cow, and Karim and I need to get back out to them. For once it isn't all about you!'

And she swept out and left Georgie reeling but angry. How dared her sister dash in and pass judgment? She was sick of them, sick of Zaraq and its so-called mysterious ways that only applied when was convenient.

And Ibrahim was sick of it too.

'They are the rules!' Karim roared. 'Only a king can change them. If you love her, then you stay in London. You have the rest of the world to be the prince of your choice, but here, in this land, you abide—'

Ibrahim could not stand to hear it said again and he interrupted with a shout of his own. 'Then I leave the land behind.'

'Ibrahim.' Karim wished it was that easy. He ached for his brother, physically. 'You are a royal prince of *this* land—our people are sick. Hassan is with his new baby, he has a fever…' He saw his brother's appalled expression. 'He will be okay, but he was a little premature. Hassan should be there for him. The king is in England, I am needed in the desert. Can you really walk away now we need you to be the ruler you were born to be?'

'I am not walking away.' Ibrahim's voice was hoarse, realisation hitting him. He was being asked to step in and he met that challenge. 'Of course I will stay while I am needed, and our father will return when he hears the news.'

'That may not be possible. I have spoken with advisors—they suggest closing the airports.'

'Fine,' Ibrahim said. 'I will step in as leader.' But as leader Ibrahim had rules of his own and spelt them out. 'Georgie will be by my side.'

'No,' Karim said, for it was impossible.

'She is mine now,' Ibrahim said, because for once the rules worked for him. After all, he had slept with her in the desert.

'She can never be yours.' Karim took no pleasure in delivering the news, no relish in revealing the secret his wife had shared with him the other night. 'She is married.' He watched darkness descend on his brother.

'No.'

'She is divorced, but….' Ibrahim closed his eyes as his brother continued. 'You know that does not count here. She cannot live with you here—she cannot be your bride.' Every word was like a hammer on his flesh but still Ibrahim stood. He sought a solution.

'She can wait for me in London.'

'As our mother waits for our father?' Karim asked. 'Would you really do that to Georgie?'

Ibrahim shook his head. 'Then do the right thing by her.' Karim suppressed a roar. 'End it with her properly—end it now so there can be no doubt in her mind.'

CHAPTER ELEVEN

'WILL you take care of Azizah for me?' Felicity asked when Karim said it was time for them to leave.

'Are you sure I'm responsible enough?' Georgie responded tartly, but she could not sustain her anger, for she knew how much being apart from Azizah would hurt Felicity. 'She'll be fine.' Georgie said and she took her sister in her arms and gave her a cuddle. For the first time she felt like the older one. 'She'll be completely fine.'

'I'm sorry.' Felicity was, but Georgie didn't need her to be.

'I hurt you,' Georgie said. 'All those years I was sick, I know how much it hurt you, and I was too weak then and too fragile for you to say how you felt. I'm not now.' She gave her sister a smile. 'Better out than in, so they say.'

'Felicity,' Karim called, and as together as Georgie felt, she didn't go out and face her brother-in-law just yet.

'You'd better go.'

'There's my milk…'

'I know,' Georgie soothed. 'You just head out there and do what you have to do without worrying.'

'I really am sorry...' Felicity shivered '...for all the things I said.'

'They've no doubt been building for a long time,' Georgie said. 'We're fine now and you don't have to worry about Azizah and neither do you have to worry about me any more.'

Except Felicity knew that she did have to worry, at least for a little while longer. She could see her husband's clenched jaw and Ibrahim's stern features and knew that Ibrahim had been told.

A fully dressed, blushing Georgie forced herself out of her room to say farewell to Karim and Felicity and she and Ibrahim stood in silence as they watched the helicopter leave.

'I must get back to Azizah,' Georgie said. 'How long will the drive take?'

'A helicopter is being sent.' He did not, could not, look at her. 'I need to get back to the people as soon as possible.' He felt it descend then, the weight of responsibility. 'I am to stand in as ruler. Decisions need to be made swiftly. There will be a lot of anxiety, a lot of unrest.'

'You'll be wonderful,' Georgie said, and went to touch his arm, but he moved it away. 'I'll help in any way I can.'

'You?' He could not keep the mirth from his voice.

'Yes, me.'

'A four-week course and you're an expert suddenly in the ways of the desert?'

She couldn't understand the change in him. 'I wasn't applying for the job of your advisor!' Georgie snapped back at him. 'So I'm good enough to sleep with, but not good enough to stand by your side.'

'The people would never accept it.'

'Oh, please.' Georgie was sick of it. 'The people don't mind Felicity.' She let out a mocking laugh. 'Oh, yes, but she was pregnant with a possible heir.' She watched as Ibrahim briefly closed his eyes, his strong features paling a touch at how very careless they had been. 'I'm not going to fall pregnant. Don't panic. I'm on the Pill.'

'Of course you are.' And that was the bit for Ibrahim that hurt, really hurt. This was a girl who carried condoms in her make-up bag for just in case, who waited on the street outside nightclubs. This was the divorced woman who could not be his princess, and he was angry, and it showed. 'Don't tell me—you're on the Pill for medical reasons.'

She could have slapped him.

Gone was the tender man who had held her. Back now was the scathing one and she didn't understand why. As the helicopter hovered, as she turned her head and covered her eyes with a scarf, as they ran beneath the blades and climbed inside and Georgie put on her headphones, she watched the tent where they had found each other disappear in the distance, and all too soon she saw the palace come into view, but not once did he look at her, not once did he attempt conversation.

As they stepped out and walked to the palace, he still refused to communicate. Elders and advisors were waiting for him and Georgie stood in the hallway a moment as Rina spoke in rapid Arabic, unsure how to behave without Ibrahim or Felicity to guide her. Briefly he glanced in her direction and only then did he speak.

'She asks if you want a room next to Azizah. If they should move your things?'

'Please.' Georgie nodded. 'Can you tell her for me?'

'Of course.' He spoke to Rina and to another maid for a brief moment, and then he turned back to her.

'All is taken care of. I have asked that they move *Ms* Anderson's things.' He hissed the word so savagely that there could be no mistake. He had been told that she had been married, and for a second she was angry at her sister for telling Karim, but she knew the fury was misdirected.

She was angry at herself.

As for Ibrahim, he still hoped his brother was mistaken, wanted her to tell him he was wrong. 'Is it Miss or Ms?'

'*Ms.*' She croaked the word out, then tore her eyes away, but not quickly enough to miss his look of disgust.

It should have been she who told him first. At least she could have explained things better. Now, looking at his cold black eyes, Georgie wondered if she'd ever get that chance. 'Ibrahim…' There were people everywhere, there was nothing she could say, but she willed him to give her one moment of his time, willed him to pull her aside, for a chance to explain, but he gave her nothing. 'Can we talk? Just for a moment.'

'Talk?' Ibrahim sneered. 'I have nothing to talk about with you—there is nothing to discuss.

'And never can there be.'

CHAPTER TWELVE

It was the longest day.

All Georgie wanted to do was throw herself on the bed, curl up into a ball, hide and grieve and cry and mourn, but there was Azizah to think of.

Azizah, who hated the bottle that wasn't her mum, who wasn't used to the bonier arms of her aunt and cried through the afternoon and long, long into the evening.

Georgie had been pacing the floor with her and had finally sat in the family lounge, where Felicity often did, and Azizah had at last given in, taking the bottle she hated and almost, *almost* falling asleep, until Ibrahim returned from a visit to the army barracks. It wasn't just her heart that leapt at the sound of him. Hassan, the prince first in line, did too. He came pounding down the corridor to greet his brother.

'You should have consulted me!' Hassan was furious. Georgie could hear them arguing as she sat in the lounge. When Ibrahim had returned she had wanted to flee, but the baby had just been settling and she'd sat as the argument had spilled into the living room.

'You should have spoken with me before closing the airports.'

'You were with your wife and son,' Ibrahim pointed out. 'You are needed there. I am more than capable of dealing with this.'

'You have closed the airports, cancelled surgery.'

'Excuse me,' Georgie said, and perhaps it was poor form to interrupt two princes when the country was in crisis, but the palace was big enough for them to take their argument elsewhere and a restless Azizah was just closing her eyes. 'She's almost asleep.'

'Then take her to the nursery,' Ibrahim snapped, and it was face him or flee. As Hassan took the phone from a worried maid, Georgie chose to face him, turned her blue eyes on him and refused not to meet his gaze.

'Hard day at the office, darling?' she said in a voice that was sweet but laced with acid. 'Should I make the children disappear?'

'Just you,' Ibrahim hissed, because it was hell seeing her and not being able to have her, hell having dared to almost love her and then to find out what she had done. 'I wish *you* would disappear.'

'It is our father.' Hassan handed him the phone. 'It is you he wishes to speak to.'

And now would have been an ideal time to leave, to slip away, as Ibrahim wished she would, except Georgie wanted to hear, wanted to be there, even if he'd rather she wasn't.

She could hear the king's angry voice even from across the lounge, and though Hassan was pacing,

Ibrahim was calm, his voice firm when he responded to his father.

'I took advice,' was his curt response, but when that clearly didn't appease his father, he elaborated. 'I took advice from experts. You have known about this for days apparently and did little.' She could see a pulse leaping in his neck. It was the only indication of his inner turmoil as he stood up to the king. 'The priority is the people,' he interrupted, 'not your flight schedule and certainly not Hassan's ego. His mind is on his newborn son, where it should be, where it can be, because there is another prince more than capable of stepping in. I have spoken with our soldiers, and the army is to open a field hospital to the west. Flights will remain grounded till we are happy this virus is contained. If you move for an exemption from the flight ban, if you feel I am not capable, then of course you must return,' Ibrahim said, and then his voice rose slightly in warning. 'And if you do, I will hand the reins back to you.' For a second his eyes flicked to Georgie. 'And I will leave Zaraq on your incoming plane.'

'You—' he spoke to Hassan when the call had concluded '—either take over completely or leave it to me. I am not ringing the hospital and waiting while they pull you from the nursery to make my decisions.' He eyed his brother. 'What is it to be?'

'The people need—'

'The people need strong leadership,' Ibrahim said. 'Which I am more than capable of providing. If you think otherwise, I suggest you ring Jamal and tell her a helicopter is taking you out to the west tomorrow, as is my schedule, to see first hand how this illness has affected our people.' He did not relent, he did not appease, he was direct and he was brutal. 'And perhaps you should check with the pediatrician. We have all been immunized, of course, and if that proves ineffective there are anti-virals, but I would check if they want you in contact with a premature newborn.'

Georgie watched as Hassan paled.

'So what is it to be?' Ibrahim pushed. 'Because if I'm not needed I'm heading for the casino.' And he would, Georgie knew. He'd head too to another woman, any woman. He was angry and she had provoked it.

'You have my full support,' Hassan said. 'And I thank you for stepping in. I am going to visit my wife and son.'

He nodded goodnight to Georgie and a now sleeping Azizah and finally they were alone.

'That was low,' Georgie said.

'That was common sense.' Ibrahim snapped. 'I don't care how safe it is, how effective the immunisation is, if it were my newborn…' And he looked at where Georgie sat holding a baby, and he was black with anger, because that morning he had almost envisaged it, not a wife and a baby but a future with someone who was not a stranger to his heart. The role of prince and a return to the desert had seemed manageable with her by his side. 'I have to work.' He turned to go, but she called him.

'Can we please talk, Ibrahim?

'I don't wish to talk to you.'

'Please.' Georgie said. 'It was something that happened a long time ago, something—'

'That cannot be undone,' Ibrahim interrupted.

'When did you become so perfect?' Georgie asked. 'I don't get why everything has to change.'

'Because it has.'

'It was a few weeks,' Georgie said. 'I was nineteen. It was hell at home and I'd lost my job when I got sick again…' She tumbled out words when he didn't respond immediately, argued her case while she still had a chance. 'I thought he was nice.'

'So you married him because he was *nice*.'

'There are worse reasons. He was older, he seemed safe, but I see now that he was a drunk like my father. I see now I just ran straight to the same thing.'

'You think that makes it better. That you tossed everything away for some middle-aged drunk.'

'It was ages ago,' Georgie said. 'I know it's frowned on here but in London—'

'I am a royal prince!' Ibrahim struggled to keep his voice down, for the sake of the baby.

'Not when you're there.' And she watched lines mar his forehead, his hand going up to his face in a gesture of frustration. He was saving her from herself and that she didn't understand. He thought of his mother, sitting by the phone, waiting. Of a life married to a man who could not always be there, who had children scattered by both geography and allegiance, and he must not, Ibrahim told himself, do that to Georgie. So instead he did as his brother had suggested, said words that would leave her in no doubt.

'I'm a royal prince,' Ibrahim said again. 'Which means…' He swallowed before continuing, but she didn't see it, just heard his low, even voice as he very clearly stated his case. 'I don't have to deal in damaged goods.' If she hadn't been holding Azizah Georgie would have stood and slapped him, but instead her eyes left his face and she sat holding the baby for comfort, holding her sweet, warm body as she chilled inside. 'The bride that will be chosen for me will know what is expected. A bride fit for my side is not found outside nightclubs with a smorgasbord of contraception and her divorce papers in her bedside drawer. If you want me to look you up in London, if you're bored one night—'

'Never!'

'Then…' Ibrahim shrugged '…we're done.'

'You're a bastard.'

'When I choose to be.' Ibrahim shrugged again. He heard her shocked silence and little Azizah start to whimper.

'Would you do as you suggested earlier and disappear with the baby?' Ibrahim said. 'I've got a country to run.'

CHAPTER THIRTEEN

I<small>T DID</small> not abate.

Not for a single minute.

There were demands and there were questions and he dealt with each and every one.

He flew deep into the desert and witnessed the suffering, then returned to have his competence questioned by a hungry press.

He did not care about tourism was his surly response at the conference.

And anyway, he questioned the questioners, did the tourists want to visit an empty desert—a ghost town of what once was?

He silenced his critics with his performance, yet for Ibrahim there was no respite, for each night he slept alone.

He went for the phone on several occasions, but it wasn't just sex he wanted. For the first time it was someone else's opinion he craved.

One other person's opinion.

'I tell him he does well.' Home from the hospital before her baby, Jamal sat at breakfast and spoke in broken English to Georgie, when Ibrahim made a surprise appearance one morning. She spoke for a little while longer to Ibrahim then turned and smiled at Georgie. 'Soon Felicity back.'

'How soon?' Georgie asked, her eyes jerking to Ibrahim, because she wanted to leave so badly, because even if she hardly saw him, just the occasional passing on the stairs, where the greeting was polite and cool had been hard enough. Now that he was sitting at the table, it was almost more than she could bear.

'Karim called and said the situation is much improved—he wants her to come home, though he will stay out there.'

'And the airports?' Georgie asked.

'I'm meeting with the doctors today. They are proposing that all visitors be vaccinated…but…' He paused, waited for her to fill in, to offer her thoughts, but Georgie didn't. 'Once the new guidelines are in place, there seems no reason not to reopen them.'

'How soon?' Georgie asked, because she did not want a debate, just answers.

'Perhaps as early as tomorrow.' Ibrahim selected a fruit from the platter, then changed his mind and Georgie looked down and saw the pomegranate. She could have picked it up herself, could have taunted him a little, but she was too bruised and raw to play games: she just wanted to go home.

'You stay till I bring the baby home,' Jamal said—the future king would not be named for some time yet. 'It will be a good day.'

Georgie gave a noncommittal smile and when the maid came to tell Hassan and Jamal that the car was ready to take them to the hospital, Georgie stood to leave too, but Ibrahim halted her.

'Will you stay when Felicity gets here?'

'Why?'

'As Jamal said, the baby will be home soon and with the illness receding, there will be much celebration.'

'I don't really feel like celebrating.'

'You could have time with your sister.'

'Not this visit.' Georgie gave a shrug and went to leave.

'Georgie.'

'What?'

'Maybe we should talk…'

'About what?'

He didn't know, but he was aching for her.

'Maybe tonight, when the palace is quiet, you could come—'

'As I said,' Georgie hissed, 'never.' And she went to walk out but he called her back and she was more angry than she had ever been in her life, because he thought he could summon her, that sex might soothe the heartache; angry too, that she was considering it.

'Georgie, you do not walk out—'

'Am I supposed to curtsey?' she hurled back at him.

'You do not leave till you're excused.'

'Oh, I've already been excused,' Georgie responded.

'When you called me damaged goods, Ibrahim, you excused me for life.'

'Like it or not, we are here together.' He just wanted to talk, but she was too angry to see that.

'Not for much longer,' Georgie snarled. 'Felicity's back tomorrow.'

'We still don't know about the airports.'

'I'll swim home if I have to.' Georgie said, and she meant it, absolutely she meant it. At the very least she would check into a hotel.

She spent the day packing, in-between looking after Azizah. She did everything she could to keep him from her mind, but as night crept in, she gave in a little and fed her craving—watched the news reports, flicking channels, because sometimes there were subtitles, and even if she didn't understand completely, there was no denying that the young prince had stepped in and brought calm. His deep voice soothed the troubled nation. Difficult decisions, it seemed, were effortlessly made, but they had taken their toll.

She could see that.

Did everyone notice the clench of his jaw as he listened to questions, or the tiny fan of new lines around those dark Zaraq eyes? Did they see that those magnificent cheekbones had become more accentuated in these past days, or the taut lines of his shoulders?

Or did only love make those details visible?

And she changed channel and changed it again, but it made no difference, because even if she closed her eyes, his face was still there and, yes, very unfortunately for Georgie, she loved him.

'Oh!' She jumped as he walked into the lounge. It was close to ten but still early for Ibrahim to be back and she had wrongly assumed the interview she was watching was live. 'I thought you were…' She gestured to the television. 'I'll say goodnight.'

'You don't have to hide in your room.'

She felt safer there, but didn't say that. She simply didn't answer, just walked past the sofa, but he caught her wrist.

'Did you understand what was being said?' He glanced over at his own image on the screen.

'Not really.'

'Things are improving.'

'That's good.' She could feel his fingers on her skin, feel the pull to join him, to sit, but she stood. 'I saw the news earlier.' She still couldn't look at him. 'There were subtitles…they were talking about the young prince, what a magnificent job you were doing…' She watched her tears fall on his fingers. 'There was talk of a bride…'

'There is always talk of marriage,' Ibrahim started, but the plight was real, he could not lie. 'If I am here as a prince, if I stay…'

'There's no if.' Georgie was angry. 'You've had your taste of power and now you want more.'

'No.' He wished it was that simple. 'It is not about power, it is not about want. I am *their* prince. The people have been patient while I grew up, but now it is time to accept the responsibility, all of it…' He looked at the television screen, the arguments, the raised voices. 'Do you understand what is being said?'

'No.'

'That is one of the elders. He asks if our rulers do care, why is there no hospital on the west side? Why does it take five days to get aid? Zaraq is rich, yet its people suffer.'

'It's changing, though.' Georgie swallowed. 'There are outreach programmes, there is a hospital—'

'That they cannot access.' Ibrahim looked at her. 'They choose to be isolated—that is what the journalist is saying now. They make us promise not to invade their desert, not to take away their ways… It is complicated.'

'There's no easy solution,' Georgie attempted, and then she saw his face, saw the worry and the lines and the pressure on him. 'Is there?'

'No easy one,' Ibrahim said. 'There is a need for more infrastructure. I told you my father tried once. He brought in experts but they do not understand our people's ways. There was a road planned, just in from the coastline, but it meant bridges. There were arguments…' And she started to understand. She felt it in her stomach, in her throat.

'You do, though?'

He nodded.

'I sit in London and I design elevators and pools that stretch from high-rise to high-rise and I focus on the skyline, but I have not forgotten the ground. I understand some of the magic and the science. I can see bridges that can negotiate the canyons. I can see how it can be done, in ways the people would allow, ways that would benefit them yet uphold their desire to live freely…' She watched as his analytical mind started to dream, then she turned her attention back to the screen, listened and read the subtitles as the interviewer asked if the prince would oversee the changes.

'For now,' Ibrahim had answered, 'we deal with the current issue. Then we move to ensure it never happens again.'

She looked at him, at a face that she could read, an expression that was suddenly familiar—even though he wasn't asleep, it was the face she had seen on the plane, a troubled face that spoke of inner torment.

'What's wrong, Ibrahim?' He closed his eyes to her question. 'I did see you when you stepped on the plane and you were nothing like the man that stepped off. Is this where you want to be?'

'Honestly?' Ibrahim said, and she nodded. 'I don't know. This is where I am needed.' He opened his eyes and looked to her and he was grateful that she stayed silent, that she didn't point out that she needed him too, didn't fight for her corner of his torn heart.

'When this is over,' Ibrahim said, 'when I get back…'

'You belong here.' Georgie said, because over the last days it had become clear that he did. He stood up and headed out, but as he got to the door he changed his mind. As he had in the club, he turned round and walked back to where she was still standing.

'What I said, about damaged goods…'

'Please don't say sorry,' Georgie said. 'Because I'd hate myself if I forgave you.'

'I don't expect you to forgive me and I don't expect you to understand—just know that by saying what I did, I had hoped to hurt you less in the long term.'

'Well, it didn't work,' Georgie said. 'It can never work.'

And somehow, to live the rest of her life, she had to accept that.

CHAPTER FOURTEEN

'It's not long now.' Georgie tried to soothe the little girl, but she missed her mother. 'Mummy will be home soon,' Georgie said, and instantly regretted it, because just the mention of her mother and Azizah's screams seemed to quadruple. 'Come on,' Georgie said, tired of pacing the luxurious nursery. Feeling the heat from her niece's cheeks, she unlocked the French windows and stepped out onto the balcony. The cool night air surprised Azizah into silence. 'I'll take you down to the beach tomorrow,' Georgie promised and stared into the black eyes of her niece for a moment, but she tore her gaze away, because Azizah had inherited Zaraq eyes.

Georgie felt the air still in her chest as she caught sight of Ibrahim walking on the beach, and when he looked up this time he did not dismiss her; this time he did not look away. She just stood and stared down at him. She could not see for sure, but thought he was looking right at her, unashamedly staring, as was she. She stared, not just at him but at a memory, and she knew they were both reliving the desert.

She did not move, tasted his lips in her mind as he walked slowly on, and she knew what to do.

Georgie put the sleeping babe in her cot, locked the French windows and headed back to her own room.

She did not need to turn the key in the lock—she knew he would never come to her. He had ended it, and would not be so cruel as to revoke it, no matter how much he wanted her this night.

This long night, before tomorrow, before normality returned.

Georgie knew it was their last chance to be alone, their last chance for a goodbye, but not in words.

Her last chance to thank him because, despite his cruel words, he had changed her, had shown her the beauty of her body, had taken her to a very different place.

He would be prince, so she must kiss him goodbye.

He found her in his bed and didn't humble her with questions.

He kissed her warmly along her neck down to her shoulder and then back to her neck. Then he spoke about that which was so painful they hadn't been able to speak of it before. 'I wish you had told me.'

'Why?' Georgie asked. He had thought it obvious, but as he went to answer he checked himself and Georgie answered for him. 'So you could have avoided me, so that it would never have happened.' And she felt his lips back on her neck and his strong body pressing into hers and she understood why she had chosen to keep quiet. 'So we could never have known this.'

'How do we go on now?' He turned her onto her back, made her look at him. 'Next time you are here visiting your sister and I am with my bride...' He was so cross with her, so cross because accepting his father's choice of bride might not have been great but it would have been bearable. Now, though, it would kill him.

'We'll come separately,' Georgie replied.

'Weddings, births and funerals generally only have one sitting, which means we will both be there, but separate and somehow denying this.' He could feel every inch of her skin beneath his, feel the body that belonged to him in every way but by law, and even if he wanted her, he was still angry. 'Am I to shake hands with your future husband, admire you children?' He could not, just could not envision it. 'Or are the next fifty years to be spent slipping out after the meal, hoping we meet in the gardens...' She shook her head.

'No.' Georgie said, because she couldn't live like that. And Ibrahim recalled something then. 'Was that why you stopped me? Not guilt about your sister?'

'My divorce wasn't through then. It just seemed wrong.'

'She's got a conscience too.' He spoke to the devil on his shoulder with a mixture of regret and wry humour. 'So that rules out a mistress.'

So, this was the last time. He climbed off her and then walked over and turned on every light, and she lay there as he walked back to the bed and pulled off the heavy silk sheet. Her hand moved to grab it, but then she let it go. She lay silent as his eyes roamed her body and she was shaking on the bed as she let him look, but she was shaking with desire rather than shame.

He looked at her toes and the fading henna flowers that climbed up her feet. He looked at knees and thighs till they felt like water, to her place that tomorrow would become private, to her stomach and then breasts he had tasted. Without him voicing his request, she heard it and turned round, and she felt like crying as his eyes swept her. Then she let healing tears come as he loved every fault, every bit that made Georgie.

She felt the heat from his gaze linger on her spine, then find a birthmark beneath her ribcage, and the little cluster of faded stretch marks on her hips. He etched his memories in his mind and then climbed into bed and made them with his mouth—touching her everywhere his eyes had been. She could feel his lips on her skin, her calves, her toes and back up again. He turned her over and she felt them rest on her stomach, where she had stopped him once. He took for ever, which was what they didn't have, but his mouth worked down and he explored her very slowly, till she pleaded with him to stop. She pulsed in his mouth and couldn't give any more, but still he would not relent, coaxing an orgasm so deep and intense she was scared to go there, and she knew what he was doing. Heard her voice shouting his name, as was his intention—a subliminal branding as he married her with his mouth, because as he took her over the edge, as she sobbed his name, Georgie knew she could never now go there again and not think of him.

She would always hold back for fear of calling out the wrong name.

He was so good it made her angry, so perfect and so exactly her size, yet she could never own him—would forever have to look through the windows of her mind to glimpse this.

Only now, when there was nothing left to give, did he take a whole lot more. He moved up her body and for the first time since the desert he kissed her mouth, and his eyes were open as he entered her and so too were Georgie's, scared even to blink. To remember this was her priority—because she never wanted to forget how his eyes adored hers so much as he moved deep within her. How pale her arm looked against his dark shoulders, and she tried to imprint in her mind the scent of him when aroused.

The hardest week was wiped from his mind. If he could just have her, then anything would be easy. He wanted to come, but he didn't want it to be over, so he resisted his body, and it hurt not to give in to it, because his body wanted the release she could give.

'Please,' Georgie said, because she was almost there and she wanted him with her. 'Please,' she said again, and then pressed her mouth in his shoulder because she didn't want to beg.

She felt like they were lying on quicksand and being drawn down into it, or sucked back into the vortex the desert had made them create, the world that they had when there was no one around. She would not, could not wait for him a second longer. She would not beg, but her body demanded on her behalf, for it rose beneath him and tightened around him; it beat a tune that he could never deny. And he gave in so that he could join her. Each urgent thrust took her further, not just to the edge but away from him, and both knew it. They both fanned the last flickers of orgasm from a fire that must die.

His hand moved down to her stomach and rested there and his mind lingered there and so too did Georgie's.

Hopefully it would hurt less when she was out of his arms, but she lay and tortured herself for a little while longer and Ibrahim did the same.

'What would happen if you don't take your Pill?'

'Nothing, probably.'

'But perhaps?'

'We won't find out,' Georgie said, her face burning because, yes, she had considered it. 'Because I took my Pill this morning and I'll take it tomorrow. I will not force you into a decision.' She was fragile in his arms but strong in her mind, and he loved her for it.

'If it was just for a few weeks…' Her skin was against his and he let his mind wander, explored options that would have once been unthinkable, except her body dared him to dream. 'Could there be annulment?'

'It happened.' Georgie's voice was hollow. 'You yourself said it cannot be undone.'

'But it was such a short time, there are no children… If it was a mistake, something you regret…' And then she was the bravest she had ever been, the clearest in her mind she had ever been, because even if she loved him, she was still herself.

'I don't regret it, though.' She watched his face darken.

'How can you say you don't regret it? That a marriage to some drunk, a marriage you admit was a mistake, a marriage that has cost us each other, is not something you regret?'

But she would not back down. 'I don't regret it because I've learnt from it.' Georgie's voice was a touch shaky as she struggled to hold onto her convictions. 'I've learnt from my mistakes. And once I would have said I regret it, because it's what you wanted to hear…I would have done anything to please you.'

'Because of your past we have no future…'

'Because of my past I'm a better person,' she interrupted. 'Because it taught me to say no, to walk away, to accept nothing but the best… So don't try to make me say I regret it. I'm not ashamed of my past, Ibrahim. If you are…' She rose from his bed and put on her gown. She walked when she didn't want to, because otherwise she might lie there, might bend herself into the woman he needed her to be, instead of the woman she was. 'That's your issue.'

'You'll come back soon?' Felicity asked as they sat in the car that was waiting to take them to the airport. Her sister had been shocked when, almost the second Felicity returned from the desert, Georgie said that she wanted to leave. But Georgie had stood her ground.

She needed to get away or she'd be back in his bed that very night, would be back in his bed till his virgin was found for him, and she was worth more than that, and so was his bride.

They needed to be apart to heal.

'Of course I'll be back,' Georgie said, though in her heart she didn't know how. How could she ever be here and be without him?

'And I'll be home in a few weeks.' Felicity tried to keep her voice light as the car drove away from the palace and Georgie deliberately didn't turn round.

But she couldn't stay brave at the airport when she hugged her sister.

'You'll get over him,' Felicity said when Georgie crumpled. 'You will.'

'I know I will,' Georgie said, but her heart wasn't sure.

The captain told them to look to the right after take-off for a spectacular view of the sun setting over the desert , but Georgie refused to turn her head because she didn't want to see a sunset without Ibrahim.

'Is everything okay, Miss Anderson?' the steward asked.

'Ms,' Felicity corrected him, because it was who she was, whether Ibrahim could accept it or not.

CHAPTER FIFTEEN

HE WAS in London.

Since their last night together, as surely as Georgie checked her horoscope in the morning, so too she typed 'Zaraq' into her search engine.

Clicked 'News'.

And just as she had so often, she scrolled through the latest offerings.

The illness that had crippled the country was all but over.

Hassan and Jamal had brought their baby home.

The king was pleased with his youngest son, so pleased that after a brief return home the king had again headed for the UK to resume *business*. Her eyes scanned faster than her fingers could click and though Ibrahim was often mentioned, today was not one of those days.

For four days now there had been no mention of him, but he was in London Georgie was sure, because Felicity had been vague when Georgie had tried to find out, and though there was no way she could properly explain it, her body told her so.

It was the hardest thing to continue working.

As much as her medically minded sister raised an eyebrow, as much as it didn't make logical sense, Georgie's work was more than touch, more than scent. To be effective it required a piece of herself, and as Georgie greeted her clients throughout the week, there weren't many pieces left to give.

Between each one she checked her phone, her messages, her emails.

She fed the craving that would not abate then forced herself to go on.

'I had booked a scalp massage, but tonight I have to go out.' Sophia Porter was a new client and Georgie checked carefully through the questionnaire she had filled in. 'Perhaps I should rebook, though I was hoping I could purchase something…' The woman closed her blue eyes and pressed her middle finger to her forehead. 'I suffer with migraines. I've tried so many medicines, so many different treatments.'

'Why don't you let me give you a hand massage?' Georgie offered, because it was her favourite initial contact. It was so non-invasive. It was often all her young clients would allow, but as the woman wavered, perhaps thinking Georgie was being pushy, she offered, 'Complimentary, and you can see if it helps before you buy anything.'

Sophia rested back in the chair, and Georgie prepared her oils. She had no ready-made blends, preferring to assess the client first and make her choices instinctively.

Lavender was a favourite for migraines, but sensing Sophia's anxiety she added clary sage and then a drop of marjoram, then Georgie moistened her hands with the fragrant brew and took her patient's hands.

Like a kitten who had never been let out, the woman's hands were soft, quite beautiful in fact, long fingered and exquisitely manicured, but despite Georgie's best efforts her client would not relax, asking Georgie questions. Sometimes talking relaxed people, so Georgie told Sophia she'd just got back from holiday.

'Anywhere nice?'

'My elder sister lives in Zaraq. It's an island—'

'I have heard of it.' Sophia smiled.

Georgie opened another vial and took out the dropper. Some melissa might help to help relax her client, and with scent being a key to memory, in that moment she was back in the desert. Her hands stopped working as well as they had, because they were shaking a little as she recalled him. As she paused to regroup, Sophia closed her eyes and inhaled.

'Ah, Bal-samin…' Sophia relaxed back in the chair. 'Tell me about Zaraq. Is it very beautiful?'

'Very,' Georgie admitted, and she felt the woman's hand relax as she talked and so she talked some more, told her about the endless sands and the miracle of finding a shell in the middle of a desert. She pulled gently on each finger in turn till the tension seeped out; she told her of the sky that went on for ever and the sun that beat down, feeling like a skullcap on your head, of the mad winds and strange rules, and when it hurt to recall it, when she could not speak of it and not weep, she looked up and saw her client asleep.

'My headache is gone,' Sophia said when Georgie woke her gently. Despite Georgie's protests, she insisted on paying and also purchased some melissa oil, and she gave the most enormous tip. 'You have a gift.'

'Thank you.'

'Could I book again?'

'Of course.' Georgie opened up her calendar on screen, and went to type in details from the form Sophia had filled in.

'Mrs?' Georgie checked. 'Or Ms? You didn't put your title.'

'There wasn't a box for "Queen".' Sophia said, and Georgie felt her heart still, felt as if she had been lied to. 'Put Ms. That is what I go by here—it is far easier than trying to explain.'

'You weren't here for a massage?'

'No,' Sophia admitted, 'but I will be back again—if you will have me. I really have had the most terrible headache. I never thought a massage could clear it but I was wrong.' She gave Georgie a tired smile. 'I worry about my son.'

'Have you spoken to him?'

'I have. He is here in London.' Georgie's heart leapt but only for a moment because now it was confirmed he was here, it hurt that he hadn't made any attempt to call. 'And you are every bit as beautiful as he describes, every bit as warm and as loving.'

'He's spoken about me?'

'Ibrahim is not one for confiding but, yes, finally he admitted what was on his mind. He misses you.'

'He hasn't called.'

'He worries about you,' Sophia said. 'Worries at the cruel press you will receive in Zaraq and what it will do to you.' She gave Georgie a smile. 'He saw what it did to me. I left, and for two years the press went wild about me. My husband forgave my indiscretion, the people of Zaraq did not. But I do not need their forgiveness. I have a wonderful life here, and my husband comes often.'

'But you miss it?'

Sophia gave a nonchalant shrug, 'Sometimes—but I am happy here, where I can be myself. I have told Ibrahim the same.' Sophia denied the pain in her soul and looked Georgie in the eye as she did so. Not for a second did she feel guilty for lying. All she saw was the chance to keep her son.

To avoid losing the last of her family to the desert.

For years she had pleaded with Ibrahim not to return and for many of those she had never thought he would. Yet since the wedding there had been a restlessness to him that at first she had tried to ignore, but seeing him from afar lead a county in crisis, hearing him talk about building a future for the people of Zaraq, she had been sure she had lost him—that again the desert had won.

Then he had told her about Georgie, about a woman who could never live there, a woman that he loved, and finally Sophia saw a way into the future, with a family to grow old with, with grandchildren who weren't strangers and Christmas and birthdays not taken alone.

'You can have both worlds,' she had told him. 'Don't turn your back on love. You will find a way, Ibrahim. Together you can work it out.'

And she told Georgie the same thing.

'He told me you were fragile, and of all you have been through.' And that confused Georgie, because she thought Ibrahim saw her differently. 'But you are not ill now. I can see for myself that you are strong. If the papers in Zaraq speak badly of you, you will not crumple. Anyway, as I pointed out to my son, you will be here. He can protect you, defend you… He should not let your past affect your future.'

'I don't think we've got a future.'

'I wouldn't be so sure.' Sophia smiled. 'I know how you feel, Georgie. I understand your fears, and if you need someone to talk to, if you want to talk to someone who can relate, you have my details.'

CHAPTER SIXTEEN

IT DID not abate.

There was a constant call and he tried to ignore it.

There was blackness in his heart and restlessness in his soul.

His tie choked every morning.

The city streets were crowded, the rain was filthy, but home could be here.

He had listened to his brothers, to the king, but he did not agree with them. He had listened to his mother too as she urged him not to close that door to his heart.

That he did have choices.

And he would exercise them, Ibrahim had finally decided. Home *would* be here and he could still help the people of Zaraq.

He climbed the stairs to Georgie's small office in long, deliberate strides, his mind made up and nothing could change it.

'I've got a client due any moment…' She recognised his footsteps on the stairs and did not look up because she didn't want to look at him—didn't want to see his face, didn't want another image added to what she must somehow one day erase.

'I am your appointment. I had my PA make it in her name.' The details did not matter. 'I need to see you...'

'It's better if we don't.'

'Better for who?' Ibrahim demanded. 'Do you feel better, not seeing me?' He saw her pale face, worried about her slender figure. 'We need to talk.'

'I'm not ready to talk.' She wasn't. The sight of him, the scent of him, to have him in her space, was overwhelming. She wanted to touch him, to fall in his arms, but she was scared to have to lose him all over again.

'Then don't talk, just listen.' He swallowed. 'I would be proud to have you as my wife.'

'But?' Georgie questioned.

'There is no but.'

She was quite sure there was and she didn't want to hear it, was scared to look at him and ask the question that she knew she must. So she forced her eyes upwards, saw the pain in his eyes and knew how badly she'd been missed. She made herself ask the question.

'What about my work?' She danced around the issue and yet subtly she broached it—so subtly, even Ibrahim did not realise it.

'I'm not asking you to give anything up.'

'You love that land, Ibrahim. You want to be there, I can see it, I can feel it, I know it...'

'No.'

'Yes.'

And it was true.

A curse that attached to him, that lived within him, but he could have both, of that he was sure.

'We will live here. I can return for work, to see my family, but our home will be here.'

And she wanted to say yes, she wanted so much to say yes, to fall into his arms, to accept his offer, to be his wife. Every beat of her heart propelled her to say yes, to give in to the throb of her body, but she was less impulsive now than she had once been, stronger now, and would first take care of herself.

'And I will return with you?'

He hesitated a moment before he shook his head. 'When the news comes out about your past, there will be outrage—but you will be here, I will protect you from that.'

'I don't need your protection,' Georgie said. 'Because it's not going to happen.'

'I'm offering you—'

'Half a princess, that's what you're offering me,' Georgie sneered, surprising herself at the bitterness in her own voice, but it was there, right there beneath the surface, black and angry, just like the truth beneath his shiny offer. 'Well, I'm worth more than that.'

'I will give you everything you need here.'

'But you cannot take me to your home. I cannot live there like my sister...'

'So you want a palace?' He too was bitter. 'You want all the finery?'

'Yes,' Georgie said. 'If I marry you, I want all of it.'

'You're not who I thought I knew,' Ibrahim said, but she was ready for him.

'I'm better than her,' Georgie said. 'And every day I get better. You know I'd have taken it a few months ago, hell, I'd have taken it last week. I'd have taken any crumb you offered just to be with you, but not now…'

'Hardly crumbs.' He was offering her everything he possibly could and then some—half his life spent in a plane just to be with her at night.

'I don't just want birthdays and Christmas and a husband at weekends. I don't want access arrangements with a family that hates me. I won't be an army wife to a country that won't even acknowledge me.' And she met his eyes with another demand. 'And don't ever describe me as fragile again.'

'I never have.'

But she didn't believe him.

'You don't have to protect me, or hide me from my past. I'm glad for every last mistake I've ever made because six months ago, six days ago, had you come and offered me this, I'd have taken it.

'I would have been your bride without question but not any more.

'I want you in my bed each night.

'I want the palace and the desert and sometimes I want to come back home to London,' she told him, each sentence delivered more strongly than the last.

'I want it all and I deserve it, and if you can't give it to me, if you can't share all of you, then I won't take the half that you're offering. I'm better off single, better off being able to go freely to Zaraq and see my sister and niece, better off being my own person than an exiled wife.'

'You're saying no?'

'Absolutely,' Georgie said.

'All that I can give you…'

'Save it for the wife your father picks for you, Ibrahim,' Georgie said. 'Save it for your virgin.' She almost spat at the thought of it, but she contained herself with words. 'No matter how well you *teach* her, she'll never be as good as me.'

CHAPTER SEVENTEEN

THE trouble with angry words, Georgie thought, as he stormed from her office, was that you didn't get to rehearse them.

She wanted to run after him, to reframe her words, to explain better—that she wasn't talking about sex, wasn't declaring herself as the world's best lover. Well, she was, but only to him.

And it wasn't just about sex. It was the conversations, the thoughts shared that he could surely never repeat so easily with another.

But she would not run after him, she was stronger than that.

Fragile indeed!

How dared he?

So she took to her oils and inhaled melissa, then hurled the bottle against the wall when she smelt Balsmin, just as Sophia had, because now it would always take her back to the desert.

Always.

How could Sophia stand there and tell her she was happy when her son and her grandson lay buried in the desert, when she had heard Ibrahim tell his father how she had wept at the birth of Hassan's son.

Sophia had lied and Georgie didn't blame her a bit for it.

Maybe she should go and talk to her, but honestly this time. Perhaps it might help to hear her true pain, to confirm how it felt to be half a wife, to seal the decision she had made.

CHAPTER EIGHTEEN

'You fool!' Ibrahim strode in, straight past his mother, to where his father sat. He left a trail of black energy that had his mother standing at the door fearful to go in, for, try as she might, she could no longer halt them. She could not contain the conflict between the two men she loved most.

'You dare to speak to me like that.' The king rose to defend himself. 'I am your father, I am your king.'

'You are not my king,' Ibrahim said. 'You will no longer be my king, for I am done. The knife of the family should not cut—and yet you have cut my mother out.'

'There was no choice.'

'You are king,' Ibrahim sneered. 'You get to choose. You make the rules.'

He could hear his mother crying in the hallway, but he would not stop. 'She deserves to be at home with you, not holed up in another country as some secret. She is the mother of your sons.'

'She cheated.'

'As did you!' Ibrahim challenged what no man

should. He stood and questioned the ways of old, the ways that chained him, his father, his family from a future. 'You had mistresses, many, even when you were with her...'

'I am king!' Indignant, he roared. 'Your mother had four young children. I was helping her so she could focus on the children, not have to worry herself attending to my needs...'

'What about her needs?' Ibrahim roared. 'Clearly she had them, but you were too blind to see.'

'Ibrahim, please,' Sophia begged from the hallway. 'Please, stop.'

As Georgie pulled up at Sophia's house she could see her at the door, bent over and crying, and as she climbed out, she heard raised voices and Sophia ran to her. 'He will kill him for how he is speaking. Stop him, Georgie. You must.'

But he would not stop and Georgie knew it. As with Felicity, there were too many words left unsaid, a confrontation that needed to be had, so she held Sophia's hand and listened as Ibrahim roared. 'You didn't even give her the dignity of ending it.' He shook his head in disgust at his father. 'You need to bring her home.'

'My people will not accept her and they will not respect me if I am seen to forgive her.'

'Some won't!' Ibrahim challenged. 'But there are many who will respect you a whole lot more—your son included.'

And the king looked at his youngest son, the one he could not read, the one he had accused of being the weakest when he had wept in the desert and just would not stop. The child that wept till it choked him, till he vomited, when his body should have been spent, when he should have curled up and accepted his lesson. Still Ibrahim had not, because he would not give up on what he believed in, and the king saw then the strength in his son.

'I love Georgie,' Ibrahim said. 'She will be my wife, and without her by my side, I will not return to Zaraq. I will never return and neither will our children.' He meant it. The king knew his son meant it. 'If I am to be a prince, she is to be royal—as my mother should be.'

'You can't just give it all away.'

'I just have.' There wasn't a trace of regret in his voice and Georgie closed her eyes as she listened and learnt just how much he loved her.

'You cannot just turn your back—the desert calls...'

'There is no call from the desert. The call was from my heart.'

'Don't mock the ways of old.'

'But I'm not,' Ibrahim said. 'The desert knows what it is doing, because it brought us together. It's the ruler who is blind.' He was done with his father. Now he just had to find Georgie, but even before he turned round she was there beside him and she took his hand, not just for him but because she was still intimidated by a king.

'Is this what you want for him?' the king challenged, and Georgie wasn't so strong.

'You don't have to give it up, Ibrahim. We can work something out. I know how much you love it.'

'They have to love me too,' he said, and it sounded a lot like her. 'I would be a good prince, a loyal prince. I can help them move forward and bring much-needed change, but only if they want all of me, and a part of me will always be with you.' He meant it, Georgie realised, he truly meant it. Gone was the tension and doubt. There was no fight inside him, no wrestling with himself, and without a glance backwards he walked from the house, taking Georgie with him.

'Do you realise what you've done?' Georgie asked.

'Do you?' Ibrahim checked, for the first time in his life bordering on embarrassed, because all that she wanted he could not now give her. 'You won't even be half a princess.'

'Am I yours?' Georgie asked, and he nodded. 'Are you mine?' she checked, and he closed his eyes and nodded again.

'Then I have everything.'

She looked down at his fingers coiled around hers, to the darkness and light that they made, then up to his eyes and the talent behind them—and there was her palace.

She had her prince.

EPILOGUE

'THE hard part will soon be over.'

Ibrahim meant the formal part of the wedding, but as she smiled back at him, it meant something more too.

The hard part was long over, but if it reared up again, she could face it.

Could face anything with Ibrahim by her side.

'Soon,' Ibrahim said, 'we can go to the desert.' Now he looked forward to his time there. Now he understood that it was wiser than anyone could begin to understand.

But his mind did not linger there. This night his attention was on Georgie. She didn't like the spotlight, the limelight, and he shielded her from it as best he could, and thankfully, though it was their wedding, there was another couple that dimmed the glare just a touch.

Zaraq was celebrating two happy couples today, Georgie and Ibrahim and also their king with his queen.

The people had always loved her, had mourned her son on her behalf, and now she was back, glowing and radiant. She sat at the table by his side as the king read his speech.

He was proud of his country and people and he thanked them for sharing this day, and he was thankful to his wife too, especially, he added on a whim, for her patience. Even Ibrahim managed a wry laugh and then his father looked right at him and he was proud as he thanked both his youngest and the wildest, even for rebellion, because challenge was good, the king said, it was how we learned. And he smiled at Georgie and thanked her too—because she had taught him so much.

Then the hard part was over and seemingly now they could enjoy.

Except Georgie couldn't.

She stood at the stop of the stairs, heard the beat of the music and the crowd urge them on, the procession that danced them, and his hand in hers.

'I can't do this.'

'You are doing it,' Ibrahim said, because she could walk if she wanted to and that would be enough, but he knew she was capable of much more. 'You're doing it now.'

Had the king been so jubilant at Felicity's wedding, so happy and proud?

She could see her mother, smiling, and the radiant face of Sophia, who was home now, and her sister glowing.

But more than that there was Ibrahim beside her and halfway down the steps, with him beside her, Georgie found her rhythm, found she could dance, even terribly, and still he adored her.

She was as she was, perfect to him.

Which gave her courage she had never imagined she could have.

To dance those last steps and accept the love that surrounded her and not care if she stumbled or fell, because Ibrahim was there to catch her. And she was there too for him.

She danced the zeffa, moved toward him and away from him, danced around him and beside him, felt the beat in her stomach that spread down her thighs to her toes, and now she could give in to it and then there was contact and she rested in his arms.

'Take me to the desert.'

'Soon,' Ibrahim said, because still there was duty, so they danced one more dance then two and then headed to a loaded table, where Georgie took her time to select from the lavish spread.

He watched nosy, bony fingers pick up a pomegranate, he saw the servant move in with a knife, but he took over and tore the fruit in two.

'Take me to the desert,' Georgie said, because she hadn't been there since that night and her womb ached for him.

And Ibrahim was about to remind her, but he checked himself. Yes, there was duty, except he had other priorities today. They had posed for the photos, had waved to the crowds, had feasted and danced—had done every last thing Georgie hated—and his duty was now to her.

'You can't just leave,' her mother chided, as Ibrahim spoke with the king. 'You can't leave midway through your own wedding.'

'Yes, she can.' Felicity hugged her sister as Ibrahim returned.

'What did he say?' Georgie asked, but it was too noisy for him to answer. They were supposed to dance again, and with the end in sight, she did. Out of the palace and to a waiting helicopter, and they flew into a desert that looked like an ocean and for a while there were no words, just his kisses as they flew over it.

'What did he say?' Georgie asked, when finally they were alone in the desert and she still worried that they'd caused trouble. 'What did the king say when you told him we were leaving?'

'To look after you.' Ibrahim replied. 'Which, I told him, goes without saying.'

She stepped into his tent and braced herself for servants, for Bedra, for bathing and petals and all the drama that was a royal wedding, consoling herself that in an hour or so they could escape to bed, but it was Ibrahim lighting the lanterns that led them.

'Where is everyone?'

'Gone,' Ibrahim answered. 'It's just you and me and no one waiting, no one watching to make sure we're safe...' He looked at his bride, at the broken mould that was Georgie, and he wouldn't change a single thing just to have this moment. 'Which you are.'

Safe in the desert, alone with him.

BRIDE FOR REAL
by Lynne Graham

Just when they think their hasty marriage is finished, Tally and Sander are drawn back together. But Sander has dark reasons for wanting his wife in his bed again—and Tally also has a terrible secret…

THE THORN IN HIS SIDE
by Kim Lawrence

Rafael Alejandro's unpredictable and alluring assistant, Libby Marchant, throws him completely off kilter. Soon Rafael's "no office relationships" policy is in danger of being broken—by the boss himself!

THE UNTAMED ARGENTINIAN
by Susan Stephens

What polo champion Nero Caracas wants he gets! Aloof beauty Bella Wheeler has *two* things Nero wants—the best horse in the world…and a body as pure and untouched as her snow-white ice maiden's reputation!

THE HIGHEST PRICE TO PAY
by Maisey Yates

When Ella's failing business comes wrapped up as part of Blaise Chevalier's recent takeover, he plans to discard it. Then he meets Ella! Perhaps he could have a little fun with his feisty new acquisition…

On sale from 15th July 2011
Don't miss out!

Available at WHSmith, Tesco, ASDA, Eason and all good bookshops
www.millsandboon.co.uk

MODERN

FROM DIRT TO DIAMONDS
by Julia James

Thea owes her future to a lucky encounter years ago with gorgeous Greek tycoon Angelos Petrakos. Angelos can't forget how she used him—and he'll stop at nothing to bring her down. Even seduction…

FIANCÉE FOR ONE NIGHT
by Trish Morey

Leo Zamos persuades his virtual PA Eve Carmichael to act as his fake fiancée at a business dinner. Leo assumes that Eve will be as neat and professional as her work, but Eve's every bit as tempting as her namesake…

AFTER THE GREEK AFFAIR
by Chantelle Shaw

The only woman billionaire Loukas Christakis trusts is his soon-to-be-married little sister. He's reluctantly allowed designer Belle Andersen to make the wedding dress on his private island—where he can keep an eye on her!

UNDER THE BRAZILIAN SUN
by Catherine George

No one has tempted reclusive ex racing champion Roberto de Sousa out from his mansion. Dr Katherine Lister is there to value a rare piece of art. But under Roberto's sultry gaze she feels like a priceless jewel…

On sale from 5th August 2011
Don't miss out!

Available at WHSmith, Tesco, ASDA, Eason
and all good bookshops

www.millsandboon.co.uk

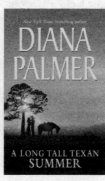
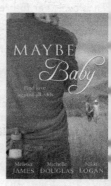

2 FREE BOOKS
AND A SURPRISE GIFT

We would like to take this opportunity to thank you for reading this Mills & Boon® book by offering you the chance to take TWO more specially selected books from the Modern™ series absolutely FREE! We're also making this offer to introduce you to the benefits of the Mills & Boon® Book Club™—

- **FREE home delivery**
- **FREE gifts and competitions**
- **FREE monthly Newsletter**
- **Exclusive Mills & Boon Book Club offers**
- **Books available before they're in the shops**

Accepting these FREE books and gift places you under no obligation to buy, you may cancel at any time, even after receiving your free books. Simply complete your details below and return the entire page to the address below. You don't even need a stamp!

YES Please send me 2 free Modern books and a surprise gift. I understand that unless you hear from me, I will receive 4 superb new books every month for just £3.30 each, postage and packing free. I am under no obligation to purchase any books and may cancel my subscription at any time. The free books and gift will be mine to keep in any case.

Ms/Mrs/Miss/Mr _____ Initials _____

_____

Surname _____

Address _____

_____

_____ Postcode _____

E-mail _____

Send this whole page to: Mills & Boon Book Club, Free Book Offer, FREEPOST NAT 10298, Richmond, TW9 1BR

Offer valid in UK only and is not available to current Mills & Boon Book Club subscribers to this series. Overseas and Eire please write for details. We reserve the right to refuse an application and applicants must be aged 18 years or over. Only one application per household. Terms and prices subject to change without notice. Offer expires 30th September 2011. As a result of this application, you may receive offers from Harlequin (UK) and other carefully selected companies. If you would prefer not to share in this opportunity please write to The Data Manager, PO Box 676, Richmond, TW9 1WU.

Mills & Boon® is a registered trademark owned by Harlequin (UK) Limited. Modern™ is being used as a trademark. The Mills & Boon® Book Club™ is being used as a trademark.